CHRISSY STEIN-MARTIN

Killer Therapy

First edition

ISBN: 979-8-9953434-0-0

This book was professionally typeset on Reedsy.
Find out more at reedsy.com

Acknowledgments

A special thank you to my beautiful granddaughter, Lily, for drawing the picture featured on the cover. Your creativity, imagination, and sweet spirit inspire me more than you know. I hope you always have the courage to stand up for yourself and for what you believe in. Never be afraid to use your voice, follow your dreams, and trust in your strength. You are deeply loved beyond measure, and I hope you never doubt your worth. The future is yours, baby girl, and I cannot wait to see all the amazing things you will do.

To all of my family, I love you Infinity Circle!

Disclaimer:

This novel is a work of fiction. While childhood events are real-life emotional truths, all character names and identifying details have been altered or fictionalized. Any resemblance to actual persons, living or dead is entirely coincidental and unintentional.

All North Carolina locations are used solely for authenticity. To the best of the authors knowledge, no actual crimes occurred at the specific locations mentioned or described.

This work explores complex and mature subject matter that may be disturbing or emotionally challenging for some readers. Reader discretion is strongly advised.

Content/Trigger Warnings:

Please note: This book includes themes including but not limited to sexual abuse, grief, drug addiction, mental illness, and references to suicide and murder. These topics are necessary to the narrative and may be distressing to some readers. Reader discretion is strongly advised.

Prologue

The cold is pressing into my face, dampness seeping through my clothes, then consciousness comes back in pieces. A dull throb at the back of my skull that pulses with every heartbeat. There is a buzzing, like a mosquito trapped in a bottle, distant rustling of air through the trees.

Where am I? The question repeats without an answer.

The memories hover just out of reach. Something happened, and the simple act of sitting up feels risky. My hand lifts on instinct finding a tender bump and warm stickiness on the back of my head. Rapid eye blinking as things begin to come into focus.

My eyes adjusting, I can make out the shape of my car and tall trees surrounding me. The trees look familiar and wrong at the same time. Their branches twisting into shapes and my thoughts do the same, half formed and slipping away.

The contents of my camera bag are spilled out onto the ground and the silence around me is deafening.

To my right, a large silhouette appears. I shift my head and clear my eyes as the image slowly comes into view.

To my shock, a large man in a brown sweater lies on the ground, face up, crimson pouring from his head and pooling onto the asphalt beneath him.

Confusion lingers but my stomach drops as his face sharpens from a blur to familiar lines.

I know him yet I don't know why he is here.

I swallow hard.

I know this man, I know his voice, I know his smile. That recognition settles into me like a threat.

Panic blooms.

I scan the area around me, my eyes snagging on small details that feels wrong in a way I can't explain. The car door to my side hangs open. The camera lenses several feet away, the scuff marks near his shoes.

I shouldn't be here.

Something tells me I didn't just stumble into this.

Chapter 1

Callie

The problem with lunch miracles is that they make everything else feel like a disappointment. Marcus and I meet at Dulcet & Delish, our favorite cozy café in Downtown Mooresville. Due to our busy work schedules, meeting for lunch on a random Tuesday afternoon would definitely be classified as a miracle.

Sitting at a little patio table, we talk about my so-called dating life which isn't really much to say other than me swiping left on dating sites and not actually dating.

As Marcus is talking, I zone out and recall the last time I actually went on a date. It was about two years ago, we met through a mutual friend at work. She tried for months to set us up before I finally agreed.

His name is Jackson.

We decided to meet for coffee and keep things very low key.

I arrived 15 minutes early because I have manners and anxiety that insist I be the first to arrive and not inconvenience others by making them wait for me. I get my coffee, then find a table near the front door for an easy get away if necessary.

While scrolling through social media, waiting for him to arrive, I come across a post from an old classmate from high school. Apparently, we have a class reunion next month. I would much rather eat glass for breakfast and wash it down with gasoline than go to a high school reunion with that crowd.

The time on my phone reads 10:10 A.M. I can't believe it, is he actually going to stand me up?

Let me not over react. Sure, I have been waiting for 25 minutes but that is my fault after all for arriving so early. I'll scroll on my phone a little longer until he arrives.

A tall man with dark brown hair and broad shoulders strolls in 15 minutes later and I quickly recognize him from a photo as being Jackson.

He is not rushed or apologetic, like he is the guest speaker at an event organized just for him. He orders his drink at the counter then walks over to the table where I am sitting.

"You started without me", he said before any introductions.

His brows knitted as he gestures to my coffee cup.

"It's basic etiquette to wait for your date to arrive before ordering, it shows patience."

I blink at him, take a sip of my coffee and genuinely wait for the punchline that never comes.

"And it is basic common courtesy to arrive on time to a first date." I reply curtly, with a forced smile and an exaggerated eye roll.

Needless to say, the date ended quickly and there was no follow up for a second date.

Meanwhile, Marcus can't stop talking about his new relationship. He and his boyfriend, Jordan, have been dating for three months, which apparently qualifies as serious now.

According to Marcus they are talking about moving in together. I smile and nod at the appropriate time while wondering to myself if I have ever felt that confident about anything in my life. His big beautiful smile tugs me back to the conversation and back to his happy moment. I can't think of anything else I rather be doing at this exact moment.

Marcus orders the hummus plate and I get the chicken salad sandwich.

I can never decide on which one to order. Marcus always orders the opposite of what I get so I can have both. He slides the hummus toward me the second it arrives, like it was always meant to be shared. No hesitation. No keeping score. Just simple, quiet generosity.

He is so good to me. A true friend. The kind of friend who pays attention to the small things and always remembers them.

Between bites, he fills me in on his relationship.

They're talking about getting a dog. He lights up when he says it, already imagining morning walks and chewed-up shoes.

They've even started looking at houses in my neighborhood.

Marcus is talking with his hands, like he always does when he's excited, nearly knocking over his drink as he gestures across the table. I've known him long enough to recognize every expression on his face, the way his eyebrows lift when he's trying to make a point or the way his voice gets louder when he forgets the rest of the world exists.

The apartment he lives in now has a dog park, sure. But he says he loves the idea of just opening a back door and letting the dog run free in its own yard. Especially in the winter. No bundling up. No leash. Just warmth inside and a dog bounding through the grass.

I nod and smile, picturing it, the fence, the yard, the life that sounds so stable and grown-up. There's something steady about the way he talks about it, like his future is unfolding in neat, responsible steps.

Not long after we finish lunch, Marcus glances at his phone to check the time, already shifting back into the rhythm of his life.

"Sorry, but I've got to go now, the realtor will be at the house soon." He says, while standing up from his chair.

He hugs me quickly, promises to send pictures, and disappears into the back parking lot with the excitement of a man who is about to sign paperwork with his full legal name on it.

Yet, I think he is making a terrible mistake.

Chapter 2

Marcus

Callie and I met in nursing school five years ago, and have been inseparable ever since. There is something about surviving nursing school together that binds you for life.

The angry clinical instructor that terrified everyone. Studying until 3:00 A.M. for a test. Mispronounced medications, self-diagnosing our classmates and the dreaded bed baths. It's a stress and an achievement, only they can understand.

We were paired together for our bed making lab. I lean into her and whisper "I thought we were here to learn pharmacology and patient assessments, instead I'll leave here feeling emotionally defeated by a flat bed sheet."

She promptly replies with a sarcastic tone, "Oh you mean the Olympic level, wrinkle free, military grade bed making that apparently determines whether I can save a life? Nothing says future nurse like aggressively tucking hospital corners like my GPA depends on it."

She definitely said it a little too loud and assertive. Everyone in class turned to look at us, including the instructor. We glanced at each other, throw our heads back and cracked up laughing.

I knew instantly that Callie and I would become lifelong friends.

Callie has always had a habit of trusting people a little too easily. She sees the best in everyone, even when it isn't really there. Most of the time it's one of the things I admire about her, but every now and then it makes me uneasy.

Take her friend Olivia, for example. Olivia has this way of inserting herself into every part of Callie's life. If Callie makes a plan, Olivia somehow ends up involved. If Callie is upset, Olivia is the first one to show up and the last one to leave. At first it looks like loyalty, but the longer I watch them, the more it feels like something else. Like Olivia doesn't just want to be Callie's friend, she wants to be the only person Callie really relies on.

Callie, of course, doesn't see it that way. To her, Olivia is just the friend who has always been there. The one who shows up with coffee when she's had a bad day or sends long texts reminding her how much she cares. Callie calls it devotion. I sometimes wonder if it's something closer to control or obsession.

I suppose Olivia is technically my friend too, at least by association. We've spent enough time in the same rooms, shared enough conversations, laughed at the same jokes. But if I'm being honest, I mostly just tolerate her for Callie's sake.

When Olivia talks, there's always this sharp edge underneath the sweetness, like she's quietly measuring everyone in the room.

Maybe I'm reading too much into it. Or maybe I'm the only one who notices the way her smile tightens whenever someone else gets a little too close to Callie.

Chapter 3

Callie

I stay behind at the café pretending to check emails while actually just wasting time before my therapy appointment. It's a beautiful fall afternoon, the kind that feels borrowed. Like nature is apologizing in advance for what winter is about to do and I intend to enjoy it while it lasts.

Marcus doesn't know that I am going to therapy. I love that he thinks I'm confident and have it all together. I'm pretty sure he would still love me if he knew about my past but it's not a risk I am willing to take.

My therapist's office is down the street from the cafe.

I make my therapy appointment every Tuesday, since that is my scheduled day off work.

As I began walking towards the cross-walk, a strange feeling creeps in that I am being watched. I scan the streets but no one seems particularly interested in me. I brush off the feeling and keep walking. I take a brief moment to admire myself in the window, the new blonde highlights? Beautiful! My new shoulder length hair? So sassy! I'm feeling great about myself today so continue my walk with a little more pep in my step and a smile on my face.

It's then when I notice the woman walking towards me. She looks to be about twenty-one years old, with copper skin, gorgeous auburn hair that flows to her waist and vibrant green eyes. She is approximately 5 foot 10 inches tall and has legs for days. At least it looks like she does compared to my short, pudgy legs.

She says hello and asks where the nearest pharmacy is. I point her in the directions of the CVS Pharmacy on the corner. She smiles and casually walks in that direction like she has all the time in the world.

Suddenly not feeling as confident as I previously did, I turn away and continue on with my walk with a little less pep in my step.

Glancing back at my reflection one last time, I notice something horrifying in the reflection of the window and I freeze.

My eyes are immediately drawn to it. I am at a loss for words and all I can do is stare at the image in the window. My eyes widen and I look around to see if anyone else can see what I see.

The image I see in the window is me, and to my horror, I notice that I am wearing two... different... shoes.

Two different shoes!

One black bootie and one chocolate brown bootie.

I look down at my own two feet, then back up again, hoping the window will magically correct itself. Sadly, it doesn't, the shoes remain stubborn and mismatched. As if they formed a tiny, rebellious alliance against me.

Scanning the other shops on Main Street, to my despair, I don't see a store that would likely sell shoes. The option to go home and get another pair is out since I live on the other side of town.

I walk to my car praying that I have another option to wear in the trunk.

Rummaging through the papers, clothes, and empty water bottles, I fail to find another pair of shoes that match.

Tempted to get back into my car and leave, I make a mature, grounded decision.

I do not run, I do not cancel my appointment nor do I fake my disappearance. Instead, I continue my walk to the therapist office as planned like a mature, rational adult.

Chapter 4

Callie – Therapy Session

I make it to therapy ten minutes before my scheduled appointment time. No big surprise there since I am early to everything.

My therapist's name is Daniel Fox. He is somewhat attractive, if you like the smart, athletic type. The kind who probably played football in high school but also corrected the teacher's grammar in class. He wears fitted button-down shirts with the sleeves rolled just enough to show his forearms that suggest he works out regularly, but not obsessively. Everything about him feels intentional and calculated.

Daniel has this arrogance about him that I don't particularly like. As if he could have any woman he wants and is the smartest man in the room. I guess as therapists go, I do want someone confident and smart, but I still am not a fan of his.

As he steps out of the office to use the bathroom he invites me to have a seat. I sit on the oversized black leather chair with matching ottoman that is across from the chair he sits in during our sessions.

It's the kind of chair that says, you're safe here, while silently judging all of your life choices.

I cross my legs at the ankles strategically tucking one shoe behind the other, hoping to keep him from noticing my unfortunate shoe mishap today. I refuse to let him add "poor footwear decisions" to his mental file of me.

The door clicks as he returns. He settles into his chair with practiced ease, legal pad resting on his knee, pen poised but not yet moving. He studies me for half a second too long. Not intrusive. Just observant.

Daniel always initiates the conversation the same way.

"Why don't we pick up where we left off last time?"

Then a pause. Measured and intentional.

"You were telling me about the relationship you had with your parents…

Today I am ready to talk and barely let Daniel finish his sentence.

"My parents were reckless," I begin. Their lives were a string of chaotic choices and I grew up surrounded by drugs, crime, and how to cope with danger rather than being a kid.

Learning how to read the shift in someone's voice or measure the weight of silence and decipher if it was safe to come out of the room was a skill I learned early in life.

In our house it was normal to call a five-year-old girl a whore out of anger. I didn't understand why the people who were supposed to love me talked to me that way. I only understood that somehow, I must deserve it.

I learned early that love could be cruel. That safety was temporary. That if something hurt, it was probably my fault. That lesson settled deep inside me, rooting itself quietly, shaping the way I saw myself long after the words stopped echoing.

My dad was 28 and my mom was 23 when I was born, old enough to know better.

Back then, my parents would read the newspaper every morning, circling names in blue ink, studying the crime reports to see which drug dealers had been arrested the night before. They treated it like strategy, who was locked up, how long they might be held, whether bail had been set. Once they were sure someone would be sitting in a cell for a while, they would break into their house.

On nights of stealing, they would come home loud and breathless, the front door banging open as they carried in armfuls of other people's lives. Furniture dragged across the floor, jewelry dumped onto the kitchen table, purses turned upside down to shake out whatever was hidden inside, and clothes tossed in piles on the couch. The house would smell like damp air, sweat and someone else's perfume. There was always this strange mix of excitement and panic humming under everything.

Sometimes I got to go with them when they would break into houses. I would sit in the backseat while they drove with the headlights off down dark streets, whispering to each other. Inside the houses, I was told to stay quiet and "shop." That's what they called it. I'd walk through rooms that still felt lived in, family photos on the walls, dishes in the sink, beds unmade, and pick out things I wanted. One time I got a television, a video game system, and a ton of toys all from one house. It was cool in the way that free things feel cool when you're a kid. But it was also very weird. Wearing someone else's shoes, nothing really fit, and none of it really belonged to me, but it is what we did.

We lived in a small two-bedroom house surrounded by trees, the kind that blocked out the neighbors and made everything feel isolated. Security bars covered the windows, casting long shadows across the walls when car headlights passed by.

It was the week before Christmas. The tree in our living room blinked with colored lights, the ornaments reflecting red and green across the walls. Presents were wrapped in shiny paper and stacked underneath, some with bows already starting to peel at the corners.

From the outside, we probably looked like any other family getting ready for the holidays.

My mom told me to go to bed, but said I could watch TV for a while first. She was on the couch playing solitaire, flipping cards against the worn wood of the coffee table, a cigarette burning in the ashtray beside her. The room smelled like smoke and pine from the artificial tree. My dad wasn't home. He was out making a drug deal, something they talked about in low voices but never tried to hide from me.

At 9:00 PM., I turned off my television like I was told. The house fell quiet except for the soft shuffle of cards and the faint hum of the refrigerator. I lay in bed staring at the ceiling, the colored Christmas lights blinking through my doorway, not thinking that in our house, even the most normal nights could turn into something else.

Out of nowhere, I heard loud screaming and glass shattering. The sound exploded through the house, loud and violent. A second later, glass rained down on me and my bed, tiny pieces stinging my skin and crunching in my sheets. I jumped up, my heart pounding so hard it felt like it might burst.

I ran into the living room as fast as I could, looking for my mom. Before I could even reach her, men with guns and black vests that said SWAT had kicked in the front door. Cold air rushed inside behind them. The police were everywhere. Boots stomping, flashlights blinding, red dots shaking across the walls. They were yelling for us to put our hands up, their voices loud and harsh, like we were dangerous.

I remember how mean they sounded. Not careful, just angry. I couldn't understand why they were yelling at us like that. I was just a kid standing there in pajamas. At one point they even threatened to shoot our dog if we didn't put him away. He was barking and confused, nails sliding across the floor, not understanding what was happening either.

The police were laughing when they told us they had arrested my dad.

Laughing.

They said he tried to outrun them and throw the drugs and a gun out of the car window while he was driving. They said it like it was a joke, like it was entertainment. But they eventually caught him and took him to jail.

My aunt came to pick me up while they were putting my mom in the back of a police car. I remember the flashing red and blue lights reflecting off the trees and the security bars on the windows. The rest of the night feels like pieces of a broken mirror, fragments I can't fully put together. I wasn't old enough to understand everything that was happening. I just knew something really bad just happened.

Days later, after my parents were released from jail, we went back home. The house felt different before we even stepped inside. Too quiet. Too empty.

When we opened the door, almost everything was gone. The television set. The game system. Furniture. Jewelry. Clothes. Even the wrapped Christmas presents that were stacked there days before were gone. The ornaments were still hanging there, blinking like nothing had changed, but the space underneath was bare.

It looked like our life had been erased.

Someone had done to our house what my parents had done to so many others. They'd come in the night and stripped it down to bones. And for the first time, I understood what it felt like to be on the other side of that kind of loss.

That year, there were no presents. No laughter or Christmas magic.

And Santa didn't come to our house at all.

Chapter 5

Callie

Olivia and I have been friends for so long that I honestly can't remember a time when she wasn't part of my life. We've been through bad haircuts, terrible break-ups, and the kind of embarrassing teenage phases that we swore we'd never speak of again.

We met in the girl's bathroom while I was cutting gym class and she was cutting history class. I started my period and was being teased by a classmate so I decided to spend the rest of my day in the bathroom until it was time to get on the bus to go home.

Olivia just didn't like history class and didn't need a reason to skip.

She gave me her hoodie to wrap around my waist. A small gesture that I will be forever grateful.

She was there when I tried to cut my own bangs and ended up looking like my hair was attacked by a rouge pair of kitchen scissors.

Olivia laughed so hard she cried, but she still showed up the next morning with a headband and convinced me it looked "intentional."

When her first boyfriend dumped her over text, we spent the night on my bedroom floor surrounded by empty chip bags and melting ice cream, taking turns writing increasingly dramatic breakup messages she never actually sent. By morning we were laughing so hard our stomachs hurt.

Olivia has always been the bold one, the kind of person who says exactly what everyone else is thinking but is too afraid to say out loud. I've always been a little quieter, more cautious, but somehow, we balance each other out. She pulls me into the world when I'd rather hide from it, and I'm usually the one reminding her to slow down before she jumps into something reckless.

Over the years, our friendship turned into the kind that doesn't need constant explanations. We can sit in total silence and still understand what the other person is thinking. A single look across the room can start a full conversation without either of us saying a word.

No matter how messy life gets, Olivia has always been the one constant I can count on. And honestly, I wouldn't trade that kind of friendship for anything.

She moved in with me two years ago when she moved back into town. She followed her dream to be a singer, but couldn't afford the Tennessee lifestyle on a waitress budget.

I was happy to have her move in with me. My mortgage and car payment does not leave much money for shopping, and I do love to shop!

Before Olivia, it was just Tank and me. Tank is my English Bulldog. He is sixty-five pounds of chocolate colored squishiness. Even though he drools excessively and farts like it's a competitive sport, he still owns my entire heart. That sweet squishy boy has been pure joy in my life.

Olivia has always had this edge about her that I admire. She's bold, fierce, smart, everything I'm not. She has long shiny beautiful raven-colored hair to the middle of her back that frames her big brown eyes. She has anger issues and rarely smiles. Most importantly, she has a loyalty that runs deeper than she'll ever admit.

Now, she works as a bartender and waitress at the local Chili's restaurant.

She hasn't given up on her dream to be a singer, but her finances have drastically slowed things down for her. She continues to save money while living with me and occasionally singing in local bars in hopes of being discovered.

In the kitchen making spaghetti and talking about our day, we sip our wine and have a good laugh over my shoe catastrophe. I tell her about my afternoon with Marcus and about his relationship with Jordan. Olivia and Marcus don't usually talk much or hang out unless I bring everyone together. Marcus says she is too negative and judgmental to hang out with often, he can only handle her in small doses.

Tank is sleeping at my feet while I sit at the kitchen counter, his warm weight pressed against my toes, his paws twitching every now and then like he's chasing something in a dream. Olivia is at the stove, wooden spoon in hand, stirring the sauce with serious concentration. The kitchen smells like garlic and crushed tomatoes, a little too much oregano, and the sharp bite of red wine she poured in just like the lady from work said.

She's been talking about this sauce recipe for a week. Some older woman she works with, married for thirty years, swears this is the secret to keeping a man, leaned over the prep table and wrote it down for her on a napkin. Olivia couldn't wait to try it. She says the key is letting it simmer long enough to "marry the flavors." I watch her taste it, blow on the spoon, add a pinch of salt, taste it again. She wants it to be perfect.

Dinner is almost done when Olivia's boyfriend, Ryan, shows up unannounced. She can do so much better than him, I mutter to myself.

They met at her job. She said he came in one night with a few friends and sat at the bar. They flirted throughout the night until the bar closed. He didn't even give her a tip, yet she still ended up bringing him home with her for the night.

He is taking the scenic route between paychecks, if you know what I mean. You know the type of guy. His alarm goes off at noon and hits snooze. He somehow still complains that he is exhausted after playing video games all day. He's got big opinions, zero follow-through and a shocking allergy to basic responsibility.

He is good looking, I'll give him that, but his tanned skin, sculpted jaw line and piercing blue eyes don't make up for the rest of him.

Tank lifts his head when Ryan walks in but doesn't get up. Even the dog seems unimpressed by him.

Ryan leans down to kiss Olivia, a small quick peck as if he had to force the gesture. He glances at the stove. "Smells good in here." He says, already opening the fridge without asking. He grabs a beer like he stocked it himself.

Olivia lights up around him. Her shoulders relax. She laughs a little louder. She hands him a spoon to taste the sauce, watching his face for approval like she's waiting for a grade.

"It's amazing." He says, barely tasting it before taking another swig of beer.

We sit down to eat dinner. The plates are piled high with pasta, sauce spooned carefully over the top, fresh basil sprinkled like she saw in a cooking video. The candles she lit earlier flicker in the center of the table as we pass around the grated parmesan cheese.

Ryan talks. Mostly about himself. A new opportunity he's thinking about. A boss who doesn't recognize his potential. A friend who owes him money. Olivia nods along, asking questions, encouraging him, twirling pasta around her fork.

I watch the way she looks at him, like he's something special. Like he's going somewhere.

And I wonder how long it will take her to realize he isn't.

Chapter 6

Olivia

Moving home was not part of the dream. In my head, Nashville was neon lights and record deals or someone discovering me in a dive bar while I pretend not to care.

Coming back wasn't an easy thing to do, but it was necessary.

To be honest, I didn't come back because I failed. I came back because Callie sounded different on the phone. You don't notice unless you know her. Callie has this bright, bubbly default setting. But on the phone, there was a hesitation. Like she was waiting for permission to finish her own sentence.

Callie thinks she needed me for the mortgage. That's adorable. She forgets I know her. I know the way she apologizes when someone bumps into her. I know the way she shrinks herself for other people. I know how she reads the room then prioritizes others feelings over her own.

So, Callie thinks I couldn't make it. Let her.

It's easier than telling her I heard the crack in her voice.

When I moved back, I told her it was only temporary until I could get back on my feet. Two years later and I'm still here.

Being Callie's protector started as an instinct. We've been friends since middle school. She has always been softer than me. The kind of person that thinks everyone means well.

At first, protecting her meant small things like making sure she made it home after work. Sitting close enough at a bar so no one tried something stupid. Somewhere along the way it stopped being something I did. It became who I was.

We are just about to eat dinner when Ryan knocks on the door. I knew he was coming over but didn't mention it to Callie.

She has never told me, but I can tell that she does not like me dating Ryan. When he comes around, she is a little more quiet and more distant.

I know he isn't someone I'll spend the rest of my life with, but for now he's fun. Being around him is easy in a way most relationships aren't. There are no heavy conversations about the future, no pressure to define what we are or where things are going. We go out, laugh, waste time together, and then go our separate ways.

I don't feel like I have to prove anything to him, which might be the best part. He never asks a million questions about where I've been or what I'm doing when we're not together. If I don't answer a text for hours, he just shrugs it off the next time he sees me. No suspicion. No interrogation.

Let's face it, he isn't exactly the brightest crayon in the box. He's the type who believes almost anything you tell him as long as you say it confidently enough. Sometimes he'll laugh at a joke a full five seconds after everyone else because it took him that long to get it. But in its own strange way, that simplicity makes things easier.

Sometimes I need space. Time to disappear for a while without having to explain myself or justify every little thing I do. With him, I can do that. I can slip away, turn off my phone, and exist in my own quiet world for a while without raising any questions. And right now, that kind of freedom is exactly what I need.

Chapter 7

Callie –Therapy Session

As expected, I am several minutes early for my appointment. Daniel motions me into the office and tells me to get comfortable.

He is just finishing up his lunch and explains he will be with me soon. Daniel walks out of the room to rinse his bowl and wash his hands.

His office is small and quaint with two over-sized, floor-to-ceiling windows facing the street. There is a small brown distressed wooden desk in the corner just big enough for his laptop, a lamp and a few essential files within reach. To the right of the desk there is a matching bookshelf full of neatly arranged psychology books, some cleaning supplies, a potted plant and a framed picture.

The frame is a gold metal frame that holds a 5x7 photo. The couple looks happy. The man in the photo is clearly my therapist about 5 years younger than he is now. In the picture he has his arm around a petite woman whose features are very ordinary.

The woman is wearing a tan turtleneck blouse and studded pearl earrings. She doesn't appear to be wearing much makeup but does wear oversized black square framed glasses. Her thin, straight brown, shoulder length hair falls neatly around her face. Her wide smile makes her appear proud and content with her life.

The phone rings, taking my focus off of the picture, when Daniel enters the room to answer it. It sounds like someone wanting to schedule an appointment.

After a brief series of yeses and noes, he writes the name "Olivia" down in his appointment book for next Wednesday morning. The name obviously gets my attention, but I don't put much thought into it. Just a coincidence, I'm sure.

My eyes are drawn back to the woman in the picture. I feel like I have seen her before, but can't figure out where I might know her from. Oddly enough, I have never noticed the picture there before.

Daniel interrupts my thought as he asks me to pick up where we left off last time.

So, I begin... Education wasn't a priority in our home.

Mom would let me stay home from school if she wasn't feeling good or if she had errands to run and didn't want to go alone.

My parents taught me things like how to roll a blunt and the difference between a nickel, dime or quarter bags of weed, before they ever helped me with my homework.

We didn't go to the dentist if we had a toothache. Instead, they showed me how to rub cocaine on the tooth or hold rum against it until the pain dulled.

At the age of 13, our family was in a car accident causing me to be hospitalized for three weeks. During that time, I got my very first toothbrush. It was then that the CNA's encouraged me to brush my teeth twice a day. Until then, I thought brushing teeth was something only adults did.

We moved around a lot growing up. After every eviction, Dad would clog the toilet with a tennis ball as retaliation. The tennis balls would cause a severe blockage resulting in expensive plumbing repairs. Apparently, not paying the rent as agreed then getting evicted was the landlord's fault.

Also, as an experienced electrician, my dad was able to connect the power straight from the transformer box outside of the house to his grow lamps in the garage. This help prevent him from being caught growing marijuana plants. The police would investigate homes with excessive power usage for illicit activities. It worked for a while but he was eventually caught and arrested. That time he spent more than a year in prison.

Even things that should have scared my parents into change, barely slowed them down. We were robbed many times while they were selling drugs. For most of my life, it was just marijuana, though they sold cocaine and pain pills at times as well.

One Wednesday morning at 10:30, a loud knock echoed through the house. My mom opened the door without checking who it was, something I would replay in my mind a thousand times later.

The man forced his way inside the house, with a gun pressed hard against her stomach. He wore dark sunglasses but no mask, he knew we couldn't call the police.

Before I could react, he turned the gun on me, the cold metal pressing against my temple. My heart stuttered. My legs felt like they might give out.

"Drugs, money, and jewelry. Now," he demanded, his voice low and steady, like this was routine.

We did everything he said.

He ordered us to the ground, face down, hands trembling as he yanked them behind our backs and tied them tight. The floor feeling cold against my cheek. I focused on my breathing, trying not to panic, trying not to move.

Then, just like that, he was gone.

The front door slammed. Silence swallowed the house.

He left with everything he came for, and the terrifying freedom of knowing he got away with it.

Once again, my dad wasn't there, leaving Mom and me terrified to handle it on our own.

Still, things were not all bad growing up. I don't recall ever missing a meal. We always had a roof over our heads, even if it meant we were living with relatives. I may not have been taught to brush my teeth, but I always had clean clothes to wear.

Compliments were not something my parents gave out. I don't remember hearing, *"I'm proud of you"* or *"you're beautiful"* or even *"I love you."* Those words just weren't part of the language in our house. Praise didn't float through the air and affection wasn't spoken out loud.

But I did have a nightly routine. Giving them a kiss on the cheek and bedtime at 9:00 P.M. And in that small ritual, I understood there was love. Imperfect, unspoken, and shaped by the limits of their own upbringing. They loved me in the only way they knew how.

When I was young, I got glimpses of something different during sleepovers at my cousin's house. Their home felt softer somehow. Quieter in a different way. I would watch as they were tucked into bed, blankets pulled up to their chins. I'd hear their parents say, "I love you", like it was the most natural sentence in the world. A kiss on the forehead and a gentle "sweet dreams."

I remember lying there in the dark afterward, wide awake.

But I understood, even as a child, how powerful words could be. Not jealous exactly, just aware.

And I would memorize it. The tone. The softness. The ease of it.

I knew it even back then, lying awake in the dark in someone else's house, listening to words that felt foreign and beautiful.

If I ever had children of my own, they would never have to guess.

They would never lie in bed wondering if they were loved. They would never search my face for approval or try to decode silence. They would never have to build proof from routines or read between the lines of what wasn't said.

I would tell them. Out loud and every day, in the kitchen, in the car, at bedtime and for no reason at all.

I would tell them I loved them until the words felt ordinary, until they carried them the way other kids carried lunchboxes and backpacks, something steady and dependable. I would tell them I was proud of them not just when they achieved something big, but when they were kind, or brave, or simply trying their best.

They would grow up certain. Certain that they were wanted. Certain that they were enough. Certain that love wasn't something you had to earn or interpret.

Even as a child, I knew how powerful those words could be.

Chapter 8

Marcus

Eight months before nursing school started, I moved to North Carolina from South Florida. My brother, Terrance and I lived together in a little town called Homestead. The town sits right between Miami and Key Largo.

Homestead is where farmland meets flip-flops. One minute you're passing endless nurseries selling exotic plants, next you're five minutes from the entrance to Everglades National Park. It's a place where your neighbor casually owns three mango trees, two pitbulls, and an airboat that hasn't run since 2004.

Terrance is two years older than me. Other than the obvious height difference, we could pass as identical twins. We both have the same dark brown eyes, a dimple in our chin and the same light brown skin tone. He has always been the responsible, polite brother and I have always had more of a rebellious streak.

We were raised by our mom, who worked two jobs.

Dad left when I was a year old and forced my mom to raise us alone. She dated a little when we were younger, but nothing ever lasted. Working two jobs to put food on the table didn't leave much time for dating, she would often tell us.

We lived in a small duplex in a rough part of town. The kind of neighborhood people drove through quickly with their doors locked and their windows rolled up. The paint on the house had long since started to peel, and the narrow patch of lawn in front was more dirt than grass.

At night, the sounds of the neighborhood never really stopped. Gunshots would sometimes crack through the air in the distance, followed by the wail of police sirens cutting through the darkness. After a while, those noises stopped feeling shocking and started feeling normal, just another part of the background like traffic or barking dogs.

Streetlights flickered outside our window, casting an orange glow that never quite reached the sidewalk. People came and went at strange hours, car doors slamming, voices arguing somewhere down the block. Sometimes music played too loud from a passing car, bass rattling the thin walls of the duplex before fading into the distance.

Inside, the walls were thin enough that we could hear the neighbors on the other side arguing about money, about work, and about things that sounded like the same fight repeating every week.

It wasn't the kind of place most people would choose to live, but it was what we had. And when you grow up in a place like that, you learn pretty quickly how to ignore the noise, how to pretend the chaos outside your window isn't something you should be afraid of.

Mom cleaned homes during the day and worked as a certified nursing assistant in the evening at a nursing home, leaving Terrance to look after me. He helped me with my homework after school and made me peanut butter and jelly sandwiches for dinner most nights. Some nights I would get bologna and cheese sandwiches and that was a treat.

We usually stayed up late watching television and playing video games since Mom wasn't there to tell us to go to bed. But she was always there to wake us up in the morning with a nice breakfast before we started our day.

When Mom got sick, Terrance and I cared for her at home. Her health declined quickly, making it difficult for her to do simple tasks like cooking and dressing herself.

I was 19 years old when she passed away, leaving me to figure out a life without her in it.

That's when the rebellion began.

Grief didn't break me quietly.

It detonated.

I stopped answering calls. Started running with people who didn't fear taking risks. I chased distraction the way some people chase salvation. Fast, and reckless. Every bad decision felt like a dare to a universe that had already taken too much.

I moved here to North Carolina to get away from the hurricanes and the bad decisions I made over the course of my life.

Terrance stayed behind, rooted in the wreckage we grew up in.

I told myself moving here would be a clean break. A reset. A chance to outrun the weather and the version of myself I barely recognized.

Chapter 9

Callie

Shopping at Molly Malone's Boutique for a cute new outfit is the highlight of my afternoon. Browsing the dresses, I choose a couple options then go to the dressing room to try them on. While reaching for the blue midi dress, I hear the door chime when someone comes into the store. I listen to the women chit chatting about nothing particular while I slip back into my jeans and sweater.

Opening the curtain, I step out of the dressing room and put the green dress back on the rack. I decide to keep the blue dress and begin looking for matching earrings and shoes. Not finding a pair of shoes to match, I make my way to the jewelry rack.

Grabbing the blue and silver hoops, I notice a woman standing across the store looking right at me. She looks familiar but I don't know her name or where I know her from. She's likely just a patient at the doctor's office I work at, so I smile to be polite. She does not return the gesture, instead she frowns at me.

Feeling uncomfortable, I turn my attention back to the earrings and pretend not to notice her following me with her eyes as I walk around the table.

I glance at her from time to time to see if she's still watching me, pretending to browse while my mind is somewhere else. That's when I catch movement just outside the window.

It's Jordan. And the man he is with definitely isn't Marcus. He is with someone I have never seen before. Maybe, it's a co-worker or family member, I think to myself.

They slow near the glass, talking and laughing.

My stomach tightens and suddenly I'm not shopping anymore, I'm investigating.

Trying to look casual, I gather my things and head to the register to pay.

I walk out of the door, and briskly head to my car. I glance over my shoulder to the boutique window and notice Jordan and his friend still standing there, and standing a bit too close for my liking.

Pressing the button on my key fob, the door unlocks.

Flustered, I jump into the seat and quickly lock the car door, I don't want them to see me.

I sit there, pretending to scroll on my phone, but really, I'm watching them.

My heart pounds as they shift positions in front of the window.

And then I see it.

Their hands intertwined.

Not an accidental brush. Holding hands.

I knew it. I knew Jordan couldn't be trusted.

Determined to confront him, I immediately get back out of my car and begin walking over to him and the unknown man he is with.

When Jordan sees me walking in his direction, he quickly drops the other man's hand.

Frowning at me, he says "Hey Callie, what are you doing here?"

I make it known that I am very upset by what I see and I give him the opportunity to tell Marcus about it before I do.

We end things on a bitter note before I walk back to the direction of my car.

While walking to my car, I remember Olivia asking me to pick up some computer paper while I was out shopping today, so I decide to run into Staples a few doors down from where Jordan is standing.

Getting distracted by the gel pens, I shop the pen isle for way longer than necessary before grabbing the computer paper that I originally came inside for.

I peek out of the door, but don't see Jordan or his friend anywhere in sight. Then head back to my car again.

Before I make it all the way back to my car, I notice the passenger side window is shattered and my car has been completely ransacked.

Who could have done this? Is this Jordan's way of warning me not to say anything to Marcus or something random?

I don't notice anything particular missing, but call and make a police report anyway.

Chapter 10

Callie – Therapy Session

As I sit down in the deep, leather chair it exhales beneath me like it remembers every confession ever whispered in this room. The smell of sandalwood and old books hangs in the air.

My eyes drift towards the bookshelf behind his desk, scanning the shelves for the gold picture frame I spotted last time I was here in this office. I need to see the woman in the picture again. I need to figure out where I have seen her before.

But the space where the frame sat is empty now. Just a faint rectangular outline in the dust.

"What happened to the framed picture on your shelf." I say carefully, watching his face instead of the shelf now. "The gold frame with you and a woman?" Daniel doesn't even blink, "I don't know what you are referring to," he claims.

He leans back into his chair, steepling his fingers like he's the calm one and I am the unstable one. Technically, that's probably pretty accurate. But, why would he remove it and more importantly, why would he lie about it?

He clears his throat and changes the subject with seamless control.

"How have things been since our last session," he asks. He feels that I seem a little stressed and on edge.

Of course I'm on edge. I feel like I am being followed lately. Like someone is just out of sight. Close enough to see me but far enough away to disappear when I turn around. Or am I just being paranoid like Marcus said?

Maybe that's what everyone thinks.

He wouldn't understand what it is like to be a woman moving through the world like prey.

Some men scan rooms the way hunters scan the woods. They look for the quiet ones. The polite girls that won't cause a scene.

He has never had a man purposely stand too close in the line of a grocery store so he can brush against your ass. Or had a man be too aggressive at a bar, then make threats when you respectfully decline his advances. That subtle flash in their eyes, where rejection becomes a challenge.

He has never been scared to be alone on an elevator with a man or calculate the distance to an exit.

And Daniel asks if I have ever tried the "grounding techniques."

He doesn't know what it's like to have an ex-boyfriend stalk you for months because it wasn't over until he said it was over. Constantly leaving threatening notes and flattening my car tires in the middle of the night. Never knowing if he was going to make good on a threat or when he might appear again.

He has never quit a job due to being sexually harassed by your attorney boss just to be told by your dad that as an attractive girl you have to expect that type of attention and you can't keep quitting jobs just because you don't like it.

Daniel studies me for a long moment before asking about my parents. About the relationship I have with them now, whether we ever managed to work past our issues.

The question hangs in the air longer than it should.

I hesitate. My fingers curl tightly in my lap. "We didn't," I finally say, my voice thinner than I intend. "We never got the chance."

He frowns slightly, confused. So, I give him the truth.

"My Mom died. Heart attack." The words come out flat and rehearsed from years of saying them without feeling. And three years later, my dad… I swallow. "Motorcycle accident."

Daniel leans forward, his curiosity sharpening. That must have been sudden. Were you there when…

"I don't want to talk about it." The edge in my voice surprises even me.

He studies my face, clearly sensing there's more buried beneath the surface. More than two tragic headlines. His eyes narrow slightly, as if he's trying to piece together something I haven't said.

But I hold his gaze, willing the door shut.

Some things are better left unopened.

Chapter 11

Daniel

I have been seeing Callie, a 29-year-old female, once a week for four weeks as a patient. In those weeks, we have primarily discussed the relationship she had with her parents growing up. Her childhood was not the norm and the stories spill out of her in careful fragments. I ask questions I already know the answers to. I ask them anyway. I can't seem to stop.

She doesn't realize how much she has already told me. Patterns repeat, it only takes a few sessions to see where to press.

Most of my days consist of listening to unhappy married couples argue about dishes, infidelity and emotional distance. Who forgot an anniversary or who stopped trying. The same tired patterns wrapped in different names.

But Callie…she's different.

Here we are at another session recapping her childhood. The clock ticks louder than usual.

I could listen to her talk for hours. Not only because of her tragedy but because of her soft voice and the pout of her lips when she is trying not to cry. The way her sad eyes search my face to see if I still believe her.

I shouldn't notice those things, but I do.

I miss this feeling. The intensity of it.

The quiet pull in my chest when she looks at me like I am the only steady thing in her life.

It's a feeling I don't get from my wife Lynn anymore.

At home, everything feels rehearsed. Predictable and dull. Lynn asks about my day without really listening to the answer. We eat dinner in silence, broken only by the television.

Callie pauses mid-sentence, twisting her fingers and whispers, "Sometimes I think it was my fault."

And there it is. The hook. The need to fix or rescue. To be the person who doesn't fail her.

I lean forward slightly, close enough to matter. I need this feeling. I need it more than I should.

I get the sense that there's something she's not telling me though, something sitting just beneath the surface of every conversation we have. It's not anything obvious, no dramatic pauses or suspicious excuses. It's more subtle than that.

Sometimes it's the way she hesitates for a split second before answering a simple question, like she's quickly deciding which version of the truth to give me. Other times it's the way her smile lingers a little too long, like she's waiting to see if I've noticed something I'm not supposed to notice.

I've caught her watching me a few times when she thought I wasn't looking. The moment our eyes meet, she always looks away too quickly, brushing it off with a casual comment or a change of subject.

There's something she's holding back.

I'm sure of it.

Chapter 12

Lynn

I hear her voice before I ever see her. My husband's voice shifts when he talks to her. It always does when he thinks someone is fragile. He's soft and invested.

Daniel has a reputation of helping broken women stitch themselves back together. He's patient and gentle. The kind of man who remembers small details and makes you feel heard.

We have been married for six years and we don't have any children. Daniel never wanted kids, saying he was too old to start. It's true he is a little older than me but still young enough to have a family. Maybe its better that way. There will be no one to come between us. No little girl to take her daddy's affection or no little boy to distract him with sports.

It will always be just the two of us, me and Daniel. There is no one else I rather spend my time with. He is my everything.

He doesn't know this but I can hear basically all of his therapy sessions through the air vents. Our apartment sits directly above his little office. The building is old, the metal vents are thin, and it carries sound more than it should.

My diagnosis of Agoraphobia makes it nearly impossible for me to have friends, much less a job. Every time I attempt to go outside my pulse increases, I feel dizzy, I sweat profusely, and get severe chest pains.

So, really, Daniel's therapy sessions are all I have.

I confess, sometimes I press my ear to the floor if they are talking too low.

Getting all of the town's gossip first hand is my only form of enjoyment.

Weekly updates on all of the town's gossip is what keeps me getting up in the morning. Tiffany and Robert have been trying for three years to have a baby. I need to know if the last IVF was a success. Has Carl stayed true to his vows and not cheat on Denise, with his ex? Will Connor find another job before his wife finds out he lost his previous job? And how is Val's alcohol recovery going?

Last year, a woman from Charlotte had been seeing Daniel about her marriage problems. On the surface, she was coming in for communication issues. That's how it always starts.

Later, I learned the truth.

Her husband had been physically abusing her since their honeymoon.

She sat in that same chair and cried to my husband like many others have.

After several months of sessions, her story ended on the evening news and she was arrested for murdering her husband.

But today is different.

Today Daniel spends the full sixty minutes fully immersed into his session with this woman. Rather than the typical 45 minutes.

Just him and a woman with a sad story.

Her voice trembles… "Sometimes I feel like it is all my fault," she cries.

Daniel's chair creeks. He leans forward when he is emotionally invested. I know that sound too well.

And something about the way Daniel doesn't interrupt her, doesn't redirect, doesn't soften it with clinical language, makes the hairs on my arms rise.

Because I've heard this story before.

At the end of the session, I'm already at the window. The blinds tilted just enough for me to see the sidewalk.

I am impatiently waiting, when she makes a slow exit from his office and casually walks towards the crosswalk.

She is a short blonde woman with an hourglass figure. She's wearing a fitted black cable knit sweater, and skinny jeans with wedge booties. The booties look to be two different colors but that's probably just the way the sun reflects off of them.

She continues walking toward the crosswalk, I can only see her from behind until she crosses the street and turns right towards her car.

And when I see who Daniel's patient is, something old and bitter wakes up inside of me.

Chapter 13

Chapter 13

Marcus

As I am leaving the hospital after my third twelve-hour shift in a row, I get a text message from Jordan. He can't stop apologizing for going out with someone else. He wants to make it up to me, he says, and invites me to dinner. I lie and tell him "I'm still waiting for my relief at work and I don't know how late it will be before I leave the hospital."

I don't tell him that I am off work and already in my car. I have more important things to worry about than Jordan, right now.

Callie's house is a little out of the way but it's important that I go by her house without her knowing that I am coming by.

Usually, Callie confides in me about everything. The big things, the small things, and all the messy details in between. If she has an argument with someone, I hear about it within the hour. If she's unsure about a decision, she calls me before she makes it. She's always looking for my reaction, my opinion, some kind of reassurance that she's doing the right thing.

And honestly, I don't mind. Our lives have been so intertwined for so long that it almost feels natural. We rarely go more than three days without seeing each other. If we do, one of us eventually sends the same message: "Are you still alive?" followed by some sarcastic comment that turns into a plan to meet up.

But lately, something has felt... off.

It's subtle, but noticeable if you know Callie the way I do. Her texts have gotten shorter. She'll disappear for a day or two without explanation, then come back like nothing happened. When we do talk, she seems distracted, like part of her mind is somewhere else.

She still laughs at the same jokes and tells the same kinds of stories, but there's a distance there that wasn't there before. Like she's carefully choosing what to share and what to keep to herself.

And that's the part that bothers me.

She's vague in a way she never used to be. Dodges questions with half-smiles. Changes the subject too quickly and isn't being honest with me. Like when she said she was going to hang out at Dulcet & Delish for a while to check emails and enjoy the atmosphere. That's not like her. She hates working in public.

By the time I got into my car and pulled out onto Main Street she was already gone. Nowhere in sight.

She claims she isn't dating anyone but she hasn't been as available as usual.

She told me she was at home reading one night, but when I drove by her house she wasn't there. I sat there longer than I should have waiting for her to get home.

I don't know what she is hiding from me, but I know she is hiding something. And if she won't tell me the truth... I will figure it out myself.

Chapter 14

Callie

Tank and I are laying in my bed, watching reruns of Schitt's Creek when I receive a phone call from Marcus. He is driving home from work tonight and just called to check on me.

He knows Olivia is out of town a few days this week and I get nervous staying at home alone, especially at night.

Admittedly, I am more nervous and anxious the past few weeks. Not only does it feel like I am being followed, now my roommate will be out of town for a whole week. That's seven days and seven nights alone in the house.

Sure, I have Tank home with me, but he won't be any protection if someone breaks into the house. An intruder could just offer him a treat or belly rubs and he would be completely useless as a guard dog. Taking the treats and rolling over to offer them his belly.

Marcus tells me I am being paranoid. "Just lock the door", he says. "Olivia will be home before you know it, then you'll just feel silly for getting yourself all worked up. "

I press my lips together, staring at the dark hallway outside my bedroom. It's easy to be calm when you're not the one here alone.

Annoyed by his comment, I tell him I need to get off the phone to finish my laundry. We both know that's a lie. My clean clothes are still sitting in a wrinkled pile on top of the dryer, exactly where they've been for the past three days. I never put them away. He knows that. I know that he knows that. But neither of us says it.

We say our goodbyes anyway and promise to talk tomorrow.

As I reach for the remote to unmute the television, I hear an unusual sound outside of my bedroom window. Tank must hear it also because he immediately starts barking and looking towards the direction of the window.

I run to the kitchen, my bare feet slapping against the hardwood, and grab the biggest knife from the block without even thinking. My hands are shaking as I hurry back to my room. I turn off the light so whoever is outside can't see in. The room goes dark except for the faint glow from the streetlight filtering through the blinds.

Tank is still growling.

I move slowly toward the window and peek through the blinds.

And there in the small gap between the slats is an eyeball, looking directly at me.

For half a second, we just stare at each other.

Then I scream.

I stumble back, nearly dropping the knife, and fumble for my phone with trembling fingers. I call 911, my voice breaking as I try to explain what I just saw.

Tank is still unsettled but no longer barking at the window.

The police arrive quickly, red and blue lights washing over the front of the house. They search the yard with flashlights, comb through the bushes, check along the fence line. They drive slowly up and down the street.

They don't find anyone.

An officer walks through the house with me afterward, calm and reassuring. He checks every window, every lock and every door.

"Sometimes people think they see something in the dark", he says gently. "But we'll keep a police presence in the area tonight."

He tells me to call if I have any more problems, then the door closes behind him, and the flashing lights disappear down the street.

The house feels even quieter than before.

Obviously, I won't be getting much sleep tonight. My nerves are buzzing under my skin, every small sound amplified, the refrigerator kicking on, the house settling, the faint hum of traffic in the distance.

Tank, on the other hand, seems completely unbothered now. He circles twice at the foot of my bed and collapses with a dramatic sigh. Within minutes, he's snoring like a freight train, deep and steady, like nothing happened at all.

I decide to keep the knife next to me in bed. I lay it carefully on the nightstand within reach, then change my mind and slide it under the pillow instead.

The room is dark. The blinds are closed tight.

I stare at the ceiling for a long time, replaying the image of that eye in the window.

Eventually, exhaustion wins. And against my better judgment, I drift off to sleep.

Chapter 15

Callie – Therapy Session

Arriving at my appointment thirty minutes early, I decide to get a cup of coffee from Walter's Coffee Shop before I go see Daniel. The small coffee shop sits just across the street from the therapist's office, its windows glowing warmly against the gray afternoon. Military memorabilia covering the walls and fills the counter.

A soft bell jingles as I push open the door, and the rich smell of roasted coffee beans wraps around me instantly.

Inside, a few older men sit scattered around at small wooden tables, quietly talking to one another or staring down at their phones. The low hum of conversation mixes with the steady hiss of the espresso machine behind the counter. I step up to order, glancing at the menu even though I already know what I want.

"Medium coffee, two cream, four sugars," I say, my voice sounding calmer than I feel.

I cradle the warm cup in my hands and take a sip when it's finally ready, letting the heat seep into my fingers.

Casually walking across the street, I reach my destination with another 15 minutes to spare.

Sitting in the waiting room chair, the clock on the wall ticks slowly, each second pulling me closer to my appointment.

I try to focus on the coffee, on the quiet rhythm of his office, but my thoughts keep drifting back to what I'm about to talk about, and whether I'm actually ready to say it out loud.

Now sitting with Daniel, the words spill out of my mouth before I even know what I am saying…

When I was 5 years old, I spent the night at my grandma's house while my parents were in jail. My cousin, Paige, stayed the night too so we could have a sleep over. When Grandma tucked us in, she said she was taking us to church with her in the morning and I was so excited. I have never been in a church before.

I remember being excited about the possibility of seeing Jesus.

I put on my soft blue dress with the little pink flowers on it that my grandma got me from a yard sale. It was by far the prettiest thing I have ever owned. I just knew that everyone at church would love it. Grandma brushed my hair and clipped it back with two barrettes just above my ears. I borrowed a pair of white sandals from Paige then washed my face in the sink like grandma told me.

When we walked into church, I stared at the long wooden benches and the tall ceilings that seemed to stretch all the way to heaven. Everything felt big and important.

Grandma said Paige and I had to go to kid's church in a different room. Paige was a year older than me, so she went to a different classroom.

Grandma walked me to my room and opened the door. The first thing I noticed was the smell of crayons. Bright lights glowed over-head, and the colorful pictures that covered the walls. Some kids were playing and laughing while others were sitting in the small chairs at the table.

We listened to bible stories and sang songs about Jesus. When we were done singing, we were allowed to color pictures and play with the toys. I sat at the table to work on a puzzle when the teacher knelt down beside me. His name is Mr. Fields but I could call him Charles. Charles told me he liked my dress and that made me smile. He said he knew my grandma and thought she was a nice lady.

Charles said he needed help carrying the books from the library and asked if I would like to help. Naturally, I was excited to help the teacher, so I quickly got up from my chair and followed him to the library. When we got there, the books were gone. It wasn't a real library. It was just another classroom but was empty and didn't have all of the toys and kids. Charles said "someone else must have collected the books already."

Charles asked me to spin around so he could see my dress twirl. He sat down in one of the kid chairs and watched me twirl over and over. When I stumbled, he reached out to steady me then pulled me in for a hug.

I didn't know him and remember feeling unsure about the hug.

While he was hugging me, he put his hands up my dress and rubbed my bottom. He just smiled and told me how pretty I looked. My body went stiff. Something inside me knew this wasn't okay, even if I didn't have the words to explain why. Then he put his hands inside my panties and rubbed my bottom harder.

In a small quiet whisper, I said "I want my mommy".

He smiled again and told me he wouldn't hurt me. His words sounded nice but his touch didn't. He continued to rub everywhere inside my panties, not just my bottom. I stared up at him with tears blurring my vision, my fingers pressed against my lips, scared and confused.

I remember thinking that he looks like the guy from Mr. Rogers Neighborhood but I can't remember details like what he was wearing or who knocked on the classroom door that made him stop touching me.

I just remember being scared and no one telling me it wasn't my fault.

Chapter 16

Lynn

The woman walking out of my husband's office is Callie Jenkins.

This is so much worse than I expected.

Daniel does not know what she is capable of like I do.

I must do something to keep her away.

Even in the therapy room, recounting the people who hurt her, she wears her trauma like a crown. Every sob, every pause, every trembling detail gives her power. Attention wraps around her like a cloak.

She is adored.

Even broken, she is irresistible.

And then there's Olivia. Loyal, protective, ready to defend Callie without thinking, without questioning. They move through the world like survivors, seen and recognized.

Meanwhile, I move unnoticed. Invisible. I am the shadow they ignore. But shadows can stretch, and shadows can strike.

Callie's attention, her power, her fragile perfection, it makes me sick. I will not let her take what is mine. Not my husband. Not my life.

Olivia's friendship to Callie represents loyalty, something I never had. If Olivia doubts Callie for even a moment, that would be a small victory.

This apartment is a cage, yes, but cages have cracks, and shadows can slip through. I can't reach her directly yet, but I can start elsewhere.

I can whisper. I can watch. I can twist the threads in her little circle, plant tiny seeds of uncertainty, small disagreements that will grow until she doesn't notice the rot spreading beneath her feet.

I imagine their faces when the tension rises.

Olivia's hesitation.

Callie's confusion.

Daniel, caught in the middle, blind as always. I savor it before it even happens.

Patience. That is the key.

Every move must be invisible. Every reaction calculated. Every moment building toward the inevitable.

She doesn't know what I am capable of. But soon, she will.

Chapter 17

Olivia

Callie and I are curled up on the couch, my legs tucked beneath me and her head resting against the armrest. "Look at this one." I say, while scrolling through pictures on my phone. It is a picture of a seagull flying away after he stole half of my sandwich.

We were still sharing vacation stories and pictures when there is a knock at the door. I get up and look out of the peephole and see that it is Ryan. I wasn't expecting him to come by today since we just returned from vacation together. He says he left his jersey in my suitcase and just stopped by to pick it up so his mom can wash it later.

While walking to the bedroom to grab his jersey, I hear him turn on the television.

Ryan always goes straight for the remote, never asks.

"Let's see what is on the news." Of course. He says it like he lives here. Like this is *his* nightly routine. "Maybe Callie is right about him," I say quietly to myself.

I find the jersey crumpled between a hoodie and my still-unpacked shorts. It smells faintly of saltwater and sunscreen. I shake it out, fold it once, and head back toward the living room.

Before I even reach the doorway, I hear Callie shifting on the couch, small movements, the way she moves when she's irritated but trying not to show it.

Ryan doesn't notice. He never does.

Channel 9 News. Field Reporter: That's right, we are standing just outside of a local Mooresville Church, where shock and grief are settling in. We've just learned that the person found dead here today was one of the church's parishioners. Charles Fields, someone familiar to many in this community.

Behind me you can see candles and flowers left by community members who say they are still struggling to process what happened here earlier.

According to authorities, emergency crews were called to the church following reports of a tragic incident that took place right inside one of the classrooms.

Church members tell me that Charles was someone who worshiped, volunteered and was respected by those who knew him. That revelation has made this loss feel even more personal for those

gathering here tonight. Authorities say that Charles was discovered hanging from the ceiling, inside one of the classrooms when staff members arrived earlier today. Emergency crews responded quickly but he was pronounced dead at the scene.

Officials are not releasing further information at this time due to the sensitive nature of the case and out of respect for his family, but it does appear to be self-inflicted. Police do not believe there is any threat to other members of the church or to anyone in the community.

Tonight, grief counselors and clergy are expected to be available for all church members who are struggling to handle the news.

Many people here tell us the shock is compounded by the fact that this happened in a place they associate with safety, faith and community.

Ryan bursts out with a crude comment about the man's death, "He probably molested the wrong girl and her daddy got revenge," he says with a smirk on his face. "You know the reputation that church has."

The words hang in the air longer than they should. No one laughs. The whole room seems to go quiet in that uncomfortable way where everyone suddenly becomes aware of how wrong the moment feels.

I glance over at Callie just in time to see the change in her expression. Her face has gone pale, her jaw tightening like she's trying to keep her emotions from spilling over.

Callie doesn't look at anyone as she walks out of the room. Her shoulders are stiff with her arms wrapped around herself like she's trying to hold something together.

A moment later I hear her bedroom door slam down the hall, it is clear she doesn't want company.

The tension lingers in the room after she's gone. Ryan shrugs like he doesn't understand what the big deal is, but I can't shake the feeling that whatever he just said hit a nerve far deeper than any of us realized.

Chapter 18

Daniel

Lynn and I met when she was still calling herself Jenna. A brittle, frightened seventeen-year-old sitting on the edge of my leather chair as if it might swallow her whole. Her mother brought her in on a gray November afternoon, rain clinging to their coats, desperation clinging harder to her mother's voice. She said Jenna was spiraling, dangerous and unrecognizable.

Jenna never looked at me that first session. She stared at the diplomas on my wall as if they were watching her back.

Her arms were a quiet map of old injuries, careful lines hidden beneath long sleeves, even in warm weather. She didn't speak much at first. When she did, her voice was flat, almost bored, as if she were narrating someone else's life. She described her self-harm clinically, detached from it, like it was an experiment she happened to observe.

Twice a week for the first year.

Jenna didn't do well with other girls. She spoke about them with a particular tension in her jaw, fingers digging into her palms. She felt watched, judged, replaced, always on the verge of being erased. There was something feral beneath her quietness, something coiled. When she described conflicts, her eyes would sharpen in a way that didn't match her trembling hands.

By the time she turned eighteen, she had shed "Jenna" like a skin. She insisted on being called by her middle name, Lynn. She said the old name felt contaminated. I didn't argue.

We reduced the sessions to once a week then. Officially, it was progress.

Unofficially, it was when everything shifted.

Lynn had a way of sitting perfectly still for long stretches, barely blinking, and then suddenly unraveling. She would cry without warning, sobbing into her sleeves, then seconds later laugh. Not because anything was funny, but because she said the crying felt dramatic. Sometimes she would apologize for existing. Sometimes she would glare at me as though I had betrayed her in some invisible way.

Her moods didn't change… they collided.

Depression wrapped around her like fog. Anxiety lived just beneath her skin, vibrating.

I often felt as if I were trying to hold water in my hands, trying to understand something that refused to stay still. Sessions were whirlwinds, fragments of memory, sudden confessions, long silences where I could hear the faint tick of the clock and her breathing growing shallow.

And then there were the moments when she would fix her gaze on me, not at me, but through me and say, very softly, "You're the only one who doesn't leave."

The way she said it didn't feel like gratitude. It felt like something more.

When we began our relationship after she turned 18, and I was 39, I told myself I was helping her in a different way. That she needed the closeness that only I understood.

But sometimes, when she would sit in my apartment in complete silence, watching me from across the room with that same unblinking stare, I would feel the faintest chill crawl up my spine.

As if she hadn't been the only one unraveling in that office.

As if, from the very first session, she had been studying me just as carefully as I had been studying her.

And I wondered to myself, who was really the one in control?

Chapter 19

Callie – Therapy Session

Parallel parking on Main Street can be so frustrating. The street is always busy, with cars creeping along in both directions and people darting across the crosswalk without much warning. Admittedly, I am not the most skilled when it comes to parallel parking, but some people seem completely clueless about how the process works. The moment I slow down and turn on my blinker, signaling that I've found a spot, the driver behind me pulls up so close to my bumper that I barely have room to maneuver.

I pull forward a little past the empty space, trying to angle the car just right before backing in. Of course, that's when the car behind me impatiently inches forward again, as if they think I'm about to abandon the spot altogether. I take a deep breath, resisting the urge to roll down the window and explain the very basic concept of parallel parking.

That's when I see two cars pulling out of their spots a few spaces ahead. I pull forward and very easily slide into one of the vacant spots with no parallel parking necessary. I'll take that as a win today.

When I step out of my car and reach for the door, I notice a police officer sitting in his cruiser a few spots behind me and if I didn't know better, I'd swear he followed me here from my neighborhood.

Shaking the thought away, I reach for the handle and step inside the office building. The familiar quiet greets me immediately. I walk toward Daniel's office, the sound of my footsteps dull against the carpet.

A moment later, the door to Daniel's office opens and he greets me with a polite smile. After a brief exchange of words about how my morning has been, he gestures for me to come in. I step inside, taking my usual seat across from him as we begin our session...

At 10 years old, my parents and a few of their friends stayed up late partying and snorting lines of coke one Friday night. It was late, and a man named Ethan stayed the night. We didn't have a guestroom so he had to sleep on the couch.

It wasn't unusual for me to have to make and serve all of their snacks while they were entertaining their guests. It didn't matter what I was doing, they would yell my name across the house and call me in to the kitchen so I could make more coffee, make brownies or clean their mess away when they were done. Sometimes, I would spit in their drinks or purposely drag their food on the floor out of anger.

I went to bed at my normal bedtime so I didn't have to continue to serve them the entire night. I remember lying in bed at night wishing I had been adopted and that my real parents would have a change of heart and come back for me. A life with complete strangers sounded like a much better option to me at the time, than the life my parents offered.

Rats had completely taken over the house. I remember hearing my dad up at night shooting them with a BB gun.

Rats would get into everything, even up on the beds. I can still feel the rat tails on my bare skin when they would climb up on the bed at night, their tails, heavy and cold. Lingering on my flesh with a slithering sensation.

I never got used to waking up to them digging in my hair at night. Never knowing if one was going to jump out on you when you opened a cabinet door or a dresser drawer was a risk we were faced with daily.

CHAPTER 19

Something woke me from my sleep this Friday night. I felt something on my privates and immediately swatted thinking it was another rat. Moments later I felt pressure on my privates again but realized then that it was a person's hand. He whispered for me to be quiet while he continued to rub on me over my shorts. I was frozen with fear and stayed very still. He took my hand in his and placed it on his bare penis then rocked his pelvis while holding my hand in place. He slid his left hand down my shorts and rubbed me again.

I didn't say anything to him, instead I jumped straight up and went to my parent's room. I woke my mom up and told her that Ethan was in my bed touching me. Her reply was "I didn't tell him to do that". I told her that I didn't want him in my bed and asked if she would make him get out of my room but she yelled again, stating "I didn't tell him to get in your bed. Now get your ass out of my room and go back to sleep!"

I went back to my room with tears in my eyes and my body trembling, then got back into bed. Ethan was no longer in my room. I was too scared to go back to sleep and laid awake for as long as I could. A little while later, Ethan came back into my room. I closed my eyes and pretended to be asleep. He just stood over my bed watching me sleep while touching his privates. After a few minutes he left my room and to my relief he didn't come back again that night.

Still confusion comes over me.

Why was Mom mad at me? What did I do wrong?

Chapter 20

Daniel

Driving back to my apartment after an early dinner with an old college friend, I roll the windows down just enough to let the cool evening air slip inside. The sky is washed in streaks of orange and violet, the last light of day stretching long shadows across the pavement. I turn up the music, the bass vibrating through the steering wheel, and begin to sing along without caring who might see me. For a moment, it feels like the world has narrowed to the rhythm of the song and the steady hum of my engine.

The sun sinks lower, settling into an awkward position just above the horizon. Its glare spills directly into my windshield, blinding and relentless. I squint and flip the visor down, but it only helps a little. The road ahead shimmers in gold, details washed out in the brightness.

The car in front of me taps its brakes, red lights flickering through the haze. I ease my foot off the accelerator, coasting, still half-lost in the chorus.

We're moving at a steady pace along a winding stretch of road. I'm drumming my fingers against the steering wheel, really jamming now, when the car ahead suddenly slams on its brakes.

My foot flies to the brake pedal on instinct.

At first it feels like hesitation, a soft, unnatural resistance beneath my foot. Then the pedal sinks all the way to the floor with a sickening ease.

My heart rate spikes. I pump the brakes once, twice, then for a third time. "Come on," I whisper, pumping the brakes again. The pedal remains useless and flat against the floorboard.

The music keeps playing, sounding too loud and filling the car as the reality settles in.

The car accelerates downhill.

The guardrail rushes toward me.

I yank the parking brake. The car fishtails violently and my tires scream.

The world tilts...

Sky, asphalt, sky, IMPACT!

Metal slams against metal. My head snaps forward. The airbag explodes in my face with a violent white cloud of dust.

Then silence. Except for the ticking.

The slow, rhythmic ticking from under the hood.

My ears ring as I fumble with the seatbelt. My fingers are slick. I don't know if it's sweat or blood.

The hood is crumpled. The guardrail is bent inward where I hit it.

If the guardrail hadn't been there... I force the thought away.

A shadow moves across my passenger's side window.

For one split second, I think it's a stranger coming to help.

Then I see the shoes. Black Doc Martens. I know those shoes.

"Daniel?" she says calmly. As if we're in a grocery store instead of a wrecked car hanging inches from a drop into the lake.

I know her voice.

She leans down into the broken frame of my window.

Her hair is pulled back neatly. Not a strand out of place.

Then darkness comes again.

Chapter 21

Olivia

Callie kept saying she felt watched, followed, like someone was always just a few steps behind her. It was a feeling she couldn't shake. Always looking over her shoulder and not comfortable being alone. I wasn't about to stand by and let someone hurt my best friend. After all, protecting her became who I was.

Last Tuesday afternoon, when she said she was "running errands," she didn't invite me to tag along. That alone was suspicious, so I followed her to see where she was really going.

Trailing her across town wasn't easy. The traffic here is ridiculous, where did these people learn to drive? Not to mention, Callie has a lead foot and barely stops at stop signs. She just rolls through them like they're polite suggestions instead of enforceable traffic violations.

Finally, she reached her destination. Callie parked on Main Street in front of the bank. I parallel-parked a few spots back and watched from my car.

I saw her step out, cross at the crosswalk, make a right, and open the door to a therapist's office.

A therapist?

Why would Callie need to see a therapist?

That was something I needed to dig into.

I needed more information, so I called his office, kept my voice calm, and scheduled an appointment for myself like I was just another patient.

He had an opening for next Wednesday, so I took it.

The appointment itself wasn't remarkable, just him asking question after question while I stumbled through answers, lying about why I needed to see him. I fed him stories about being insecure, feeling like a failure, like a disappointment.

If I'm being honest, it wasn't much of an exaggeration. Not making it in Tennessee as a performer has weighed on me more than I realized.

It was actually kind of nice to talk to him.

Daniel offered to walk me out. I was his last appointment of the morning, and he said he was meeting someone for lunch.

As I left the session, feeling heavier than when I'd walked in, I reminded myself why I was actually there in the first place.

We parted ways at the crosswalk. I watched him get into a small black Mercedes. He sat there for a moment, fidgeting with his phone.

I climbed into my car just as he pulled away. I managed a quick U-turn and easily caught up to him.

After trailing him for 30 minutes, I see him turn into the parking lot of the doctor's office where Callie works.

He drove slowly through the lot.

Too slowly.

Daniel never got out of his car. He crept past the front entrance, then slowed again beside Callie's car. He lingered too long behind it.

I eased my car closer.

The moment he noticed me watching, Daniel sped out of the lot and turned onto Williamson Road, disappearing into traffic.

That's when I set the plan into motion.

Chapter 22

Callie

I am out having drinks with Marcus. The kind of Friday night that feels earned. A small brewery tucked into a brick corner of downtown Mooresville, low ceilings, exposed pipes, amber lights strung lazily across the bar. The place always smells faintly of hops and old wood.

Marcus was halfway through telling a story he'd already told twice before. I remember thinking how normal everything felt. Just cold glasses sweating onto paper coasters, the dull roar of conversations blending into white noise. The kind of night where you can finally unclench your jaw.

We were distressing. Letting the week slide off our shoulders.

Olivia was late.

She texted once, *"on my way."* No emoji. That wasn't like her.

When she finally walked in, the door chimed louder than usual. Or maybe I just noticed it more. She paused just inside the entrance, scanning the room too quickly, like she was making sure someone hadn't followed her in. Her coat was half-buttoned, hair slightly disheveled, lipstick smudged at the corner of her mouth as if she'd wiped it away with the back of her hand.

She looked… wrong.

Not crying. Not angry. Just shaken.

Marcus waved her over to our table.

Olivia smiled, but it didn't reach her eyes. Her pupils looked too large in the dim lighting. She sat down beside me with her knee pressed tightly against mine.

"Are you okay?" I asked.

"I'm fine", she said too quickly. "Just had words with some jerk before I left work."

Her voice was steady, but her fingers were trembling around the menu. She wasn't reading it. Just holding it.

Marcus made a joke about workplace drama. Olivia laughed on cue. She kept glancing toward the door every time it opened, every time the bell chimed.

I leaned closer. "What happened?"

She shook her head. Nothing. He just wouldn't drop it. Kept saying weird things. It's handled.

Conversation picked back up, sports, weekend plans, harmless small talk. Laughter drifted around us. Glasses clinked. Someone dropped a fork behind the bar and it hit the floor with a sharp metallic crack that made Olivia flinch hard enough to knock her knee into the table.

She finally took a long sip of her beer, like she was trying to swallow whatever had followed her inside.

We turn our attention back to the television when the crowd begins to cheer, Touchdown!

Panthers score and are in the lead 13 to 7. Fitzgerald comes on the field to attempt the extra point.

The crowd's attention is focused on the game when the game is interrupted with breaking news.

News Reporter: A fatal car accident took place Wednesday evening on Interstate 77 North, claimed the life of a 41-year-old man, authorities confirmed.

The accident occurred just past Exit 36 at approximately 9:30 p.m. when a single vehicle left the roadway and collided with a cluster of trees. The circumstances surrounding the crash remain under investigation.

Emergency crews responded to the scene and found Ethan Barnes trapped inside the heavily damaged vehicle. Firefighters worked carefully to extricate Barnes while paramedics administered emergency medical treatment at the scene.

Barnes was transported to a nearby trauma center with life-threatening injuries. Hospital officials later reported that despite extensive life-saving efforts by medical staff, he succumbed to his injuries later that evening.

Witnesses at the scene told police they observed the vehicle being driven erratically prior to the crash and believe drugs or alcohol may have been factors. However, authorities have not confirmed whether impairment contributed to the accident. Toxicology results are pending.

Police believe someone else may have been responsible for the accident and is asking for anyone who may have witnessed the crash or has information about the events leading up to it is urged to contact the Mooresville Police Department.

The investigation remains ongoing.

The words echo in my ears long after the reporter stops talking.

I'm still staring at the television, blinking rapidly, trying to make sense of what I just heard, when Marcus blurts out, "Don't you know that guy, Callie?"

My throat tightens.

The image on the screen freezes on Ethan's smiling driver's license photo, the same crooked grin he flashed when he was standing over by bed and touching himself.

I nod slowly.

Two men from my past. Two separate "accidents." Both dead within weeks. Charles found hanging in the church with unclear circumstances.

Now Ethan dies in a suspicious car accident.

A chill crawls up my spine.

What are the odds? Statistically microscopic. Two men connected to me. Both suddenly gone.

This isn't a coincidence. This is a pattern.

Am I about to become a suspect?

Who else knows of our connection?

Chapter 23

Daniel

I wake to antiseptic and the steady, mechanical beep of a heart monitor.

For a moment, I don't know where I am.

The ceiling tiles are too white. The lights are too bright. My mouth tastes like copper and something medicinal. When I try to lift my hand, it feels too heavy like it belongs to someone else.

A nurse, walking by, notices my eyes open and calls for the doctor.

"You're lucky." The doctor says, while approaching me. "Only minor cuts and bruises. And a mild concussion. "

Lucky? The word echoes strangely in my skull.

My car, however, wasn't so fortunate. The officer standing near the foot of my bed informs me it's totaled. I didn't even notice the officer walk in.

"No eyewitnesses," the officer continues. "No one has come forward. Do you remember anything about the accident?"

My head throbs when I try to think too hard. There's a ringing in my ears, like static between radio stations. I close my eyes and let the memories come.

Williamson Road. Late evening traffic. The sun low enough to glare in the windshield.

A car in front of me slams on its brakes. I slam on mine but nothing happens.

Smoke. The smell of gasoline. Airbag powder burning my lungs.

A shadow at the window. A woman's face framed in the cracked glass.

Olivia.

Her eyes weren't panicked. They were calm.

I remember trying to speak, but my tongue felt thick and useless. She leaned slightly closer, studying me, as if confirming something. Then she stepped back. I never saw her call for help. I never heard her shout.

The officer is still standing there, waiting. "Mr. Fox?" he prompts gently. Anything you can recall could help.

If I say her name, this becomes something else.

Not an accident. An accusation.

And I have no proof beyond a fractured memory and a concussion the doctor insists could distort things.

But I know what I saw. Don't I?

My head pulses harder, doubt creeping in. What if she was just a bystander? What if my brain is filling in blanks, attaching a familiar face to trauma?

Yet I can still see her expression, cold and satisfied, like she has been waiting for this moment.

The officer's pen hovers over his notepad. "Do you remember anyone at the scene?"

My throat feels dry. I swallow.

Do I tell the police?

What else does Olivia know and what is she capable of?

Chapter 24

Olivia

Daniel is a fraud. A professional manipulator, someone who hides behind a calm voice and a notebook while pulling information out of people who are too vulnerable to question him.

Trusting someone like him is a mistake waiting to happen.

Now it is time to put my plan into action.

Tampering with his brakes was easy. Too easy.

The parking garage was dim, humming with the buzz of fluorescent lights and smelling of oil, rust, and damp concrete. Water dripped somewhere in the distance, each hollow plink echoing like a countdown.

My pulse roared in my ears as I moved between the rows of cars, hoodie pulled tight around my face, every distant footstep making me freeze in place.

I told myself I was protecting Callie. That this was justified.

When I finished, I stepped back into the shadows, my breath shallow and my thoughts racing. For the first time, I wondered whether I had just saved my best friend or just crossed a line I could never uncross.

I had Googled just enough. Watched a grainy video. Waited until I knew his car would be here unattended for at least an hour while he was out to dinner with a friend. I crouched beside the driver's side wheel, fingers steady.

When I finished, I wiped down every surface I'd touched, tucked the small knife back into my bag, and stepped into the shadows between two SUVs.

My breath came shallow and fast, chest tight with adrenaline and something darker.

Had I just saved my best friend?

Or had it become something else entirely?

Chapter 25

Daniel

The alarm blares at its usual 7:30 A.M., dragging me out of sleep. My entire body aches, a dull, relentless pain radiating from the injuries I sustained in the car accident earlier this week. Every movement feels like a punishment, but I force myself out of bed and shuffle toward the bathroom.

I catch my reflection in the mirror and wince. My face is pale, my eyes rimmed with fatigue, and even the simple act of touching my own cheek sends a sharp jolt of pain through me. I frown at the bruises and bandages that seem to mock me with every glance.

The thought of a full day of patients makes my shoulders drop. I'm not sure I have the energy to face anyone today. So, one by one, I call every person in my book to reschedule their appointments for next week, my voice carefully steady despite the exhaustion. Every call feels like another drain on what little strength I have.

Except Callie. I can't cancel her. There's a pull I can't ignore. She's the one who keeps me focused when everything else blurs. Seeing her today is not just about the appointment, it's about control, about influence, about keeping her close enough that I can shape what she thinks of me.

I need her trust. I need her attention.

And in ways I can't admit even to myself, I need her to see me like this.

So, I leave her slot untouched. She's the only one who matters today, and the reason I'm willing to push through the pain.

Letting her see me like this, face bruised, arms wrapped in bandages, may actually work in my favor. In fact, it might be the most useful part of the entire situation. People trust vulnerability. They respond to it without even realizing they're doing it.

I can already imagine the shift in her expression. Concern. Curiosity. Maybe even a little sympathy. All perfectly natural reactions. Especially with her nursing background.

In therapy, trust is everything. Patients open up when they believe they're safe, when they feel like the person sitting across from them understands pain too.

Seeing me injured might make me seem more human to her, less like the quiet observer behind the notebook and more like someone who has experienced his own share of trouble.

And Callie is already vulnerable. People like her want to connect, to feel understood. If she believes she's seeing a side of me no one else does, she'll start lowering her guard without realizing it.

The bandages, the bruises, the carefully chosen explanation, it all helps build the illusion without making it too obvious.

Sometimes the easiest way to gain someone's trust is to let them think they're the one seeing the real you.

Chapter 26

Callie – Therapy Session

Today I arrive at my therapy appointment with only five minutes to spare. Traffic was worse than usual, cars backed up at every light, horns blaring and people cutting each other off.

By the time I pull into the parking space and rush through the front door, my nerves are already buzzing.

I smooth my hair as I step inside his office, trying to collect myself, but I still feel flustered and slightly out of breath.

Daniel is already sitting in his chair waiting for me. His posture is relaxed, one leg crossed over the other, a notepad resting on his knee.

At first glance everything seems normal, but then I notice his face is covered in scrapes and bruises. Dark purpling along his cheekbone, a thin cut near his eyebrow that looks like it was recently stitched. There are more marks on his arms where the sleeves of his shirt are rolled up, rough abrasions that look fresh.

Before I can even open my mouth to ask what happened, he casually says, "Car accident."

The words come out quickly, almost rehearsed, like he knew exactly what I was going to ask before I asked it.

There's a brief pause after that, the kind where it feels like more explanation should follow. But it doesn't. Daniel simply glances down at his notepad and flips it open, avoiding eye contact just long enough to make it clear he doesn't want to discuss it.

Then he clears his throat and looks back up at me with the same calm, professional expression he always wears during our sessions.

"I've got a pretty busy afternoon today," he says, tapping his pen lightly against the paper. "So, if it's okay with you, I'd like to jump right into your session."

Something about the whole exchange feels strange, but I take my usual seat in front of him and pick up where I ended last time.

Still focusing on his injuries, I push those thoughts aside and begin on a memory from when I was 16 years old.

Mike, a friend from school was having a small party at his house one Saturday afternoon. A few friends were supposed to meet there around 4:00 P.M. My dad dropped me off a little early. I was so excited to go because my parents never let me go to parties. They thought this one would be okay because it was in the afternoon.

Standing in his room scrolling through the music downloads he had on his phone, I was told to pick a song while we were waiting for everyone to arrive.

Mike lived in a boys group home with five other teenage boys. His room was small and cluttered. A metal bunk bed with messy sheets. A book shelf full of old records, a blue tooth speaker, and a collection of Simpson cartoon characters. The room smelled of stale cigarettes and dirty shoes, a smell I would remember for the rest of my life.

He came into the room and closed the door. Then he slid the dresser in front of it. The sound of the wood scraping along the baseboards still echoes in my memory.

He smiled at me and said he wanted to have fun. I said I didn't want to. I remember saying it very clearly. "I don't want to." I remember saying the word No.

Then everything slowed down. My body went numb before my mind could catch up. I didn't fight. I didn't scream. I didn't even resist. I just froze.

He pulled down his shorts then, tugged my shorts down just enough to rape me.

Why didn't I fight? Why didn't I scream? Why didn't I do anything besides allow him to have his way?

When he was done, he stood up like nothing happened. Like we had just finished studying for a test. I pulled my shorts back into place with shaky hands, trying to push away my tears before they escaped.

A few moments later he moved the dresser from the door and went out to get a drink. I cautiously followed him to the kitchen keeping a safe distance between us. I remember looking at the clock, the time was 4:23 P.M. I debated if it was too early to ask to go home because I didn't want to appear rude.

My dad was supposed to pick me up at 7:00 P.M. but I couldn't wait that long. I wanted to be anywhere else but here with him.

I said I wasn't feeling well and asked his older brother for a ride home. Without question, he drove me home. The ride home was quiet. Still in shock, I sat stiff in the front seat while he surfed through radio stations. I remember sitting there, upset at myself for not fighting back. That thought played through my head all the way home and still to this day.

The next day at school he brought me a teddy bear as if everything was okay. Like we had a consensual moment and were in a cute relationship.

Was everything okay, did I imagine it? I was so embarrassed as if it were my fault. Meanwhile he was laughing and joking with friends carefree.

Feeling foggy, unsafe and somehow responsible about what happened, I begin to cry.

My shame turned to anger and later that day I told a friend what happened. From there everything happened pretty quickly. She told the school counselor and then the police were called.

I called my mom to inform her what was going on and that the police were coming to the house to talk to me. My mom made it clear that the police could not come into the house, for obvious reasons.

So, I sat out in the police car for 30 minutes telling my story and answering all of his repetitive questions.

Scared, alone and even more shame.

Chapter 27

Callie

Allergy season is upon us. Which makes for a busier than normal day at the doctor's office. I have worked here for about three years, long enough to know the rhythm of the chaos. Long enough to recognize a sinus infection from a mile away. And long enough to appreciate that somehow, I landed the most amazing coworkers on the planet. People who can manage to inhale a protein bar in 16.2 seconds and still manage to smile while being yelled at for the long wait.

As a triage nurse the phones don't just ring, they scream. One line blinking. Then two. Then five. It's a symphony of sniffles and panic.

We go through the same gentle explanation over and over... Antibiotics don't work for viruses, they won't prevent you from getting a sinus infection, and they definitely won't fix pollen.

But sure, lets blame the person answering the call.

Meanwhile, the waiting room looks like a tissue commercial and somewhere in the distance, a printer jams for the third time.

Through it all, I sit at my desk with my headset slightly crooked, coffee already cold beside me, trying to save the world one runny nose at a time.

It's finally lunch time.

The staff gathers around the microwave to warm up their left-overs and frozen meals. Patiently waiting, I sit at the table and open Monopoly Go on my phone. Anything to mentally clock out for 5 minutes, when Monica turns on the news.

We are half-listening as the meteorologist predicts the weather for the rest of the week, even though he hasn't been right all month. Still, we listen.

The news reporter cuts in. There has been a shooting.

Local News: Police are investigating a robbery that ended in a fatality late Thursday night in Statesville.

Officers were dispatched to the parking lot of Signal Hill Mall at approximately 11:15 PM following multiple 911 calls reporting gunfire. When police arrived, they discovered one individual unresponsive at the scene. Where he was later pronounced dead by emergency medical personnel.

The caller has asked to remain anonymous and has declined to give a formal statement at this time.

Officers believe the incident began as a robbery that escalated. The victim has been identified as 30 -year-old Statesville resident, Michael Harris. No further details about the victim or the details that led up to the shooting have been released as the investigation is on-going.

The area remains secured while detectives collect evidence and interview potential witnesses. Authorities are asking anyone with information to please come forward.

The breakroom television drones on in the background, cycling through the same grim footage and bold yellow police tape.

My co-workers hover near the microwave, shaking their heads.

"What is the world coming to?"

"I hope they find the shooter soon."

"You're not safe anywhere these days."

Their voices overlap in a chorus of fear and outrage.

I sit at the small round table by the vending machines, shoulders relaxed, head tilted down at my phone, rolling dice and collecting stickers.

I make sure my face stays neutral with the appropriate amount of concern.

Inside, though?

I'm fighting a smile so wide it almost hurts and I am worried that someone will notice.

Chapter 28

Marcus

Today, I finally decide to pack up the rest of Jordan's things, carefully folding his clothes, stacking boxes, and tucking away the little reminders of him that have lingered in the apartment far too long. I want this chapter of my life closed, and forgotten.

Besides, I have a date tonight with a super cute guy I met at work, and I don't want even a hint of Jordan's presence lingering when he comes over. The thought of starting something new should be exciting, but instead my chest tightens with a mix of nerves and anticipation.

I'm halfway through a box of old books when the doorbell rings. My stomach drops. Not expecting anyone, I move cautiously to the door and peer through the peephole.

Two police officers are standing there, their faces unreadable, uniforms crisp under the afternoon light. My pulse spikes. What could they possibly want?

When I open the door, Sergeant Nash speaks first and introduces himself. With his tone serious, he says "We need to talk to you about your friend Callie Jenkins," not bothering to introduce his partner.

My heart drops with what they are about to tell me. Did she get in an accident? Or worse, is she dead?

The officer assures me that she is fine, that they need to discuss her possible connection to a few suspicious deaths that have recently occurred in the area.

The words hit me like a punch.

Callie?

What does she have to do with this? Questions spiral in my mind faster than I can catch them. Three murders, and now she's somehow involved?

My hands tighten on the edge of the doorframe, and I force myself to stay calm, though my mind is spinning. "Callie? But how," I ask the officer.

I invite the officers in and tell them to sit at the kitchen table.

officer Nash steps closer, his gaze steady, while his partner hangs back, silent but imposing. "We're trying to piece together the victims connections to her."

I swallow hard, my throat suddenly dry. Every instinct tells me to protect Callie, but the words I need to say aren't coming easily.

"Do you know Charles Fields?" the officer asks, his tone even but probing.

"No," I reply honestly, my voice a little tighter than I'd like.

He doesn't pause. "What about Ethan Barnes… or Michael Harris?"

I hesitate, blinking rapidly as my mind races to place the names. "No," I answer again, forcing my voice to stay steady. "I have never heard of them," I reply, knowing very well that Callie does have a connection to them.

The officers exchange a look, and I can feel the weight of their scrutiny pressing down, making the room feel smaller. Each name feels heavier than the last, like a reminder of just how close the recent events are to everything I care about.

Nash's eyes don't leave mine. "We just need you to be honest. Anything at all could be important."

I continue to deny any possibility that Callie could be connected in any way, my voice firm even as my mind races. No matter how many times they try to intimidate me, I refuse to give them a single detail.

After a few more pointed questions and long, unsettling stares, the two officers finally leave my apartment, walking away with no more information than they came with.

I shut the door behind them and lock it quickly, my hands shaking despite my attempt at composure. The silence that follows is suffocating.

And then the realization hits me like a punch to the gut. Callie may very well be involved in all three murders.

I replay everything I know in my head. She had a connection with Ethan Barnes. She attended the same church where Charles Fields was found. Lately, she's been distant, acting strange in ways I can't ignore.

I always knew she was keeping something from me, but I never imagined it could be something this huge. The thought twists in my stomach, a mix of fear and urgency.

I need to find Callie, before the police do.

Chapter 29

Olivia

Waking up after a great night's sleep is the best way to begin any day. Sunlight filters through the blinds, casting thin lines across the ceiling, and for the first time in days my mind feels quiet. I stretch beneath the blankets, a slow smile creeping across my face. I slept better than I have in weeks, comforted by the thought that I had finally taken care of a huge problem for Callie.

Rolling onto my side, I grab my phone from the nightstand. The screen lights up in the dim morning light as I unlock it and open the Iredell Firewire page. My thumb moves quickly, swiping through posts and headlines, searching for the one thing I know has to be there, the accident.

It doesn't take long to find it.

My heart gives a small jump as I tap the article and push myself upright against the headboard, the blanket draping around my waist while I begin to read. The glow from the screen reflects across the room as my eyes scan every line, eager for the details.

Then my stomach drops.

According to the report, the occupant of the vehicle was transported to Lake Norman Hospital after crashing into a guardrail… with **minor**

injuries.

Minor injuries?

I stare at the words, certain I must have read them wrong. My grip tightens around the phone as I reread the sentence again, slower this time.

No. It's exactly what it says.

"What in the actual hell?" I blurt out, my voice louder than I intended in the quiet house.

The room suddenly feels smaller, the satisfaction from earlier draining away and leaving behind a cold, creeping frustration. That wasn't supposed to happen, he was supposed to die.

I need to find Callie before Daniel does.

Chapter 30

Callie

After a long day at work, all I can think about is a hot shower and collapsing into bed. My shoulders ache from hunching over my desk all afternoon. I turn into my driveway and cut the engine, letting the quiet settle around me for a moment.

Then headlights flood my rearview mirror and a police cruiser pulls in behind me.

My stomach tightens as I step out of my car. An officer is already standing near the back of my car by the time I close my door.

"Callie Jenkins?" he asks. His voice is deep and serious. The kind of tone that makes it clear this isn't a casual neighborhood visit.

"Yes... that's me," I say slowly.

"We'd like to ask you a few questions concerning a few suspicious deaths that have recently happened in the area."

The word suspicious lands heavy in the cool evening air.

I glance past him at the cruiser and notice another officer sitting in the passenger seat, watching us through the windshield. He hasn't moved yet. Just observing.

"Can we talk inside the house?" the first officer asks.

I hesitate for half a second. My mind runs through possibilities. "Of course," I say, forcing a polite smile.

I walk up the short path to my front door and unlock it, aware of the officers behind me. As I step inside, I hear the passenger door of the cruiser open. The second officer follows us in.

He's much taller than the first. Broad shoulders, and hard expression on his face. While the first officer at least attempted something close to polite, the tall one looks like he's already decided something about me.

The house suddenly feels smaller and Tank seems uneasy with their presence also. He doesn't bark, just sniffs their feet and circles around their legs a few times as if he is waiting for them to decide where they are going.

"Sorry about the mess," I say automatically, even though the place is spotless. I kick off my shoes and set my purse on the kitchen counter.

My nerves start buzzing under my skin. "Would either of you like a glass of water?" I ask.

They both shake their heads. "No thank you, ma'am."

"Please have a seat," I say, pointing to the chairs at the kitchen table.

The shorter officer pulls out a chair and sits down while the taller one remains standing behind him, arms crossed, scanning the room like he's memorizing everything in it. The photos on the wall, the stack of mail on the counter, the knife block beside the stove.

Tank eventually relaxes and lies down next to my feet.

The seated officer clears his throat.

"I'm officer Nash with the Mooresville Police Department."

He reaches into his jacket and flashes a badge before setting a small notebook on the table.

"We received an anonymous tip," he continues carefully, "suggesting that you may be connected to the victims of three recent deaths in the area."

My fingers tighten around the back of the chair I'm holding.

Three deaths? Connected to me?

A strange ringing fills my ears. "I think there must be some mistake,"

I say quietly.

Sergeant Nash studies my face, like he's measuring every twitch of muscle.

"That's what we're here to find out."

Behind him, the tall officer finally speaks for the first time.

"Do you recognize the names Charles Fields… Ethan Barnes… or Michael Harris?"

The room suddenly feels very, very quiet. And for a split second, I forget how to breathe.

I answer all of their questions as calmly as I can, choosing my words carefully and sticking to the truth wherever it benefits me. I explain that I have absolutely no idea who Charles or Ethan are, repeating it more than once when Sergeant Nash circles back to their names.

"I'm sorry," I say, shaking my head. "Those names don't mean anything to me."

They exchange a look but continue.

Of course, they can connect me to Mike. There's no point pretending otherwise. "We went to school together years ago, back when everyone knew everyone". I tell them exactly that, keeping my tone casual, like it's the most normal thing in the world.

The tall officer, who still hasn't introduced himself, leans forward slightly.

"That's interesting," he says. His voice is low and flat. "Because we found your DNA in Ethan's car."

The words hang in the air between us.

"Oh," I say, letting out a small breath. "Actually… that might make sense."

Both officers watch me closely now.

"My car was broken into a few weeks ago," I explain. "Someone smashed the passenger-side window and went through the glove compartment. I reported it to the police that same day."

"Maybe whoever broke into my car was the same person you're talking about." I say in a helpful tone.

The tall officer studies my face for a long moment, like he's searching for something just beneath the surface.

Inside, I feel a small flicker of satisfaction.

Making that police report might have been the smartest decision I've made in a long time.

After a few more questions, I glance at the clock on the microwave.

"I'm really sorry," I say politely, standing from the table. "But I actually have plans tonight, and I need to start getting ready."

Sergeant Nash slowly closes his notebook and the tall officer finally straightens up from the wall.

"We'll be back in touch," he says, his voice firm. "After we check out your story."

His eyes linger on me for a second longer than necessary, like he's trying to memorize my reaction.

I force a small, polite smile. "Of course."

But as they walk out the front door and their cruiser disappears down the street, the quiet that fills the house feels heavier than before.

Because something tells me this conversation is far from over.

Chapter 31

Marcus

Trying to look inconspicuous, I park between two trucks and wait for her to arrive. I see her enter the parking lot then park her car few spaces over from mine. She doesn't seem to notice me. I had a feeling she would be here, I think to myself.

She was easy to spot since the state park is not a popular hangout spot on a regular Tuesday evening.

Sitting in my car, peering through the car windows, I can see that she is talking on the phone. Grimacing, it's fair to say she isn't enjoying the conversation. When she ends the call, she puts dark sunglasses on her face, even though it's not bright out today.

She pulls a baseball cap onto her head while sitting in her car looking around like she is waiting for someone else to arrive.

To my left I notice a man walking in the direction of my car. Is that who she is meeting? Or is he coming over to me? To my relief he is unlocking the door to the blue Dodge truck to the left of me. He hops into the truck and pulls away. Luckily, the car to the right of me is still there and is blocking her from spotting me.

After the truck pulls away, I put my attention back to her car but notice she is no longer sitting in it.

"Dang it!" I yell, as I punch the steering wheel. Where did she go?

CHAPTER 31

Looking around the parking lot I don't see her anywhere but her car is still parked in the same spot.

Not sure where to look first, I decide to walk to the trails to determine which way she may have gone.

I need to find her. This may be my only chance to find out what is really going on.

Chapter 32

Olivia

I get to the State Park approximately twenty minutes before Callie arrives.

The sky is already beginning to bruise, streaks of orange melting into violet over the lake. It's exactly the kind of evening Callie can't resist. She's predictable that way. Golden hour, calm water, silhouettes of trees. She'll be standing at the shoreline soon, camera lifted, completely absorbed.

Ryan's car hums quietly as I cut the engine.

I told him mine was in the shop. Routine maintenance. He didn't hesitate. Tossed me the keys like always. He trusts too easily. That's what makes him useful.

No one would recognize this car. No one would connect it to me.

That's when I spot him. He's parked between two oversized trucks like he is trying to disappear.

My stomach drops. What is he doing here? He doesn't even like the outdoors. Complains about bugs and dirt all of the time.

Yet there's his car. I'd recognize that dented bumper with the rainbow sticker anywhere.

My pulse races, but I force myself to breathe evenly. Maybe it's coincidence. No. I don't believe in those anymore.

I lower myself in the seat, pretending to talk on my phone while I watch from the corner of my eye.

A truck door slams beside him, loud and sudden.

He turns instinctively toward the sound, attention pulled away for just a second.

That's all I need.

I shove Ryan's door open and slip out, keeping low. Gravel crunches under my shoes but the wind rattling through the trees covers me just enough.

Don't look back. I duck behind a thick oak and risk a glance through the trees.

He's still in his car. The truck beside him pulls out of its space, tires spitting gravel. For a split second, his face turns toward Ryan's car then scans the parking lot.

My lungs burn. I force myself to move deeper, weaving between trees, heading toward the narrow footpath that runs parallel to the lake. Callie's usual spot is about a quarter mile down, near the crooked pier where the water reflects the sunset like glass.

If she's already there...

A twig snaps behind me. I freeze.

It's Callie.

Callie doesn't take pictures long before she packs up her belongings and heads back to her car. I follow a safe distance back so she can't see me.

But as I we get closer to the parking lot, one thought keeps tightening in my chest.

He's waiting for her in the parking lot. I must get to him before he gets to her.

Chapter 33

Callie

Adjusting my lens as the last stretch of golden light spills across Lake Norman. The water glows amber, rippling softly beneath a sky fading into dusk. Fall leaves drift across the shoreline and for a moment the world feels peaceful.

I exhale slowly.

This is why I come here. No phones. No questions. No dissecting my past under fluorescent lighting. Just me, my camera and the quiet hum of nature.

Walking down the path headed to the opening of the lake, I spot a family of squirrels running around the trees. I stop to get a few pictures then continue on my way.

A twig snaps behind me.

I glance over my shoulder but don't see anything and think to myself, probably the squirrels.

Then another twig snaps. Sounds like the squirrels are getting closer. Or maybe a deer?

I turn my attention back to the beautiful picturesque view over the lake. The boats and birds along with the sunset will be stunning pictures to share with friends on social media later.

Still, the feeling creeps up my spine. That prickling awareness I have learned not to ignore. The overwhelming sense of being watched. I lower my camera and scan the tree line. Nothing unusual to see, but my pulse still quickens.

I don't like the feeling so I snap a few more shots then decide to head back to my car.

I pack my camera into my bag but shaking fingers make it difficult to zip the compartments.

The parking lot is a short walk up the gravel path but the distance seems to increase the faster I walk. With only a few cars left in the parking lot I begin to feel more uneasy and increase my walk to a slow jog.

Opening the door to my car, I see him standing near the edge of the trees.

I recognize him but instantly feeling this person does not have good intentions.

A hand grabbing my arm. The metallic scent of blood. My camera hitting the ground. The sound of my own labored breath.

Then, Nothing.

Flashing red and blue lights pulls me from my drowsy state while the officer slings a series of questions at me. "Who are you? Are you hurt? Whose blood is this? Do you know him?"

My head is spinning and confusion consumes me.

The officer's voice feels like it's coming from underwater, muffled, distant, and distorted.

Another question. Another flashlight in my eyes. I flinch.

A second officer crouches beside me, speaking more gently.

"Hey, stay with us.

Can you tell me your name?"

I open my mouth, but nothing comes out. My throat burns. My tongue tastes like copper.

"I...I don't..." The words scrape out like sandpaper. "I don't know."

The officers exchange a look. Not good. Not reassuring.

To the right of them, paramedics are examining something. For a moment, I think it's another flashlight.

Then I see the dark shape on the ground.

A body.

I gasp.

It's Marcus.

Chapter 34

Lynn

I was two years old when my parents divorced and even then, I felt the shift.

My mother changed almost overnight. She traded sweat pants for tight dresses and red lipstick. She started staying out late, and rotated through men like she had an agenda.

Some of the men drank too much while others called her names. One man slapped her hard enough that I learned to recognize the silence that followed.

Then she finally met Chuck.

He was quiet and soft spoken. The kind of man who made a point to kneel and look a child in the eye to introduce himself. I was almost four when they started dating. Within a few months, we moved into his house. It was a small but beautiful house in a neighborhood where all of the neighbors waved as you walked by.

In the beginning Chuck felt like a rescue.

He would buy me so many gifts like dolls, sparkly shoes, and a pink bike with a little white basket on the front.

He told me I was special and mature for my age. Then he called me his pretty little princess and I liked that title.

Being new in the neighborhood, I didn't have any friends. My world became the house and the man who filled it.

He worked from home, which meant he was always there. He taught me how to swim, how to rollerblade, and how to ride a bike without training wheels. My mom joined us when she wasn't working, but most days it was just Chuck and me.

Long afternoons that felt golden and important.

Chuck and I had a special connection from the beginning. He said I was wise beyond my years. That I understood things other children didn't. He shared many "secrets" with me such as frustrations about my mom and private adult jokes.

Sometimes the things he did made me uncomfortable, left me feeling embarrassed and ashamed in ways I couldn't explain. I hated that part of myself that let it happen, hated that I could feel both disgust and a desperate need for his attention at the same time.

Every time, I told myself it was worth it, that if I could just hold his focus a little longer, it would mean I mattered. That tiny flicker of attention felt like the only thing that made the risk tolerable, like it justified the discomfort, the fear, and the shame.

It wasn't strength. It wasn't bravery. It was something weaker and harder to admit. A need to be seen, even if it meant letting myself be used in ways I knew I shouldn't.

I was the chosen one.

Chapter 35

Callie

By the time anyone knows her name, it isn't her real one. She introduces herself as Lynn Fox.

Soft spoken, polished, forgettable in the way fancy wallpaper is forgettable.

Back then she was Jenna Lynn Carson, the girl who sat three rows behind me in high school.

She wasn't invisible then. She was worse.

She was the girl who tried too hard to fit in. The girl who laughed too loud at everyone's jokes. The girl who told herself that if she couldn't be them, she would ruin them.

I clearly remember Jenna not liking me in school but I never understood why. She made my life hell back then.

It started small. Notes slipped through the vents of my locker, folded into sharp little triangles like weapons. *Liar. Slut. Trash. Everyone knows.* No name signed, but I knew. The handwriting was tight and pressed too hard into the paper, like she was trying to carve the words instead of write them.

Then came the rumors.

Some weren't true. Some were close enough to true to sting twice as hard. She had a talent for twisting things and taking a harmless story and turning it poisonous. A ride home from a friend became something scandalous. A bad grade became proof I was stupid. A private insecurity somehow became public knowledge.

And every time I caught her watching from three rows back, there was that same expression, that flicker of satisfaction quickly buried under innocence.

She made fun of my clothes. My hair. The way I walked. Every day it was something different. She would say it just loud enough for others to hear.

I told myself it was just high school. That she was insecure. That it would pass.

But insecurity doesn't vanish. It evolves.

And now, years later, she calls herself Lynn Fox.

But I remember Jenna, and Jenna never forgot me.

Years pass and people grow up. They change and move on.

At least that's what I told myself when I saw her name pop up online for the first time.

Softer hair, subtler makeup, a wardrobe curated for invisibility.

If you didn't know what you were looking for, you'd never connect her to Jenna Lynn Carson.

But I did, because some expressions don't change.

Chapter 36

Fortunately, Callie didn't require any medical attention. She cleaned the wound herself with quiet precision, dabbing at the blood until the edges were clean, then carefully placed a few steri-strips across the site. Satisfied, she stepped back and called it a day, her movements calm and controlled, as if the injury had barely interrupted her.

She's never been one to let anyone make a fuss over her. Even when the pain stung and the skin around the wound throbbed, she refused to complain or draw attention. It's the kind of quiet strength that commands respect without asking for it, the way she handles everything herself, no matter how inconvenient or unpleasant.

Marcus is going to be fine too. The doctors said the blow to the head looked worse than it was, lots of blood, mild concussion, just a couple staples needed but no permanent damage.

What a relief.

Still, hearing him recount the story to the police and to Callie made my stomach twist into knots. His voice shook as he described the shadow trailing him down the sidewalk, the sudden rush of footsteps behind him, the crack of something hard against his skull.

He kept touching the bandage at his temple like he couldn't quite believe it had happened.

Apparently, he had been following Callie. He said he'd noticed she had been acting distant, distracted, jumping at small noises, staring at her phone like she was waiting for something terrible. He thought she might be in trouble. He was worried about her well-being.

Just like me.

The irony makes me chuckle a little.

I stood there while he spoke, arms folded tightly so no one would see my hands trembling. I kept my expression soft and concerned, the perfect picture of sympathy.

No one questioned me. No one suspected.

I didn't confess to being the one who hit them.

The memory keeps replaying anyway. I remember the weight of the tire iron in my hand, heavier than I expected. I hadn't meant to swing that hard. I hadn't meant to hit anyone at all. I just panicked when he turned too quickly, what was he planning to do to Callie?

And when Callie started to turn around, brushing her hair off her shoulder, confusion already forming on her face, I didn't have a choice, or at least that's what I keep telling myself. If she saw me there, if she realized I had been the one following her for weeks, she would start asking questions.

Questions about Daniel and his accident, maybe. So, I swung again…

The sound was dull and final.

She crumpled beside Marcus, and for a moment the world went completely silent.

I remember thinking, *this is it.*

What did I do? I ruined everything.

I never meant for any of it to happen, not the stalking, not the lies, and definitely not my friends getting hurt.

Now Marcus is recovering. Callie is asking questions. The police are circling closer.

And I'm standing here, pretending to be afraid of the same monster I created.

Chapter 37

Lynn

My phone buzzes, and I see a call coming in. The voice on the other end says. "Hello, this is Officer Nash, can my partner and I come up to speak with you?"

I hesitate for a moment, then press the buzzer. A faint click echoes from the intercom as the door unlocks. I step back and wait, my pulse picking up as I hear footsteps approaching the stairs. What could they possibly want from me, I think to myself, already knowing the answer.

He knocks twice before I open the door and invite him in. His partner trails behind him, silent and imposing, the kind of presence that makes your skin crawl without a single word spoken. I glance at them both, trying to read intentions I can't see.

As they step into the door, I gesture for them to sit on the couch in the living room. I don't bother offering them something to drink, hoping they won't be here long enough to need one.

While getting situated on the couch he removes some pictures from his large manila folder. Laying the pictures on the tables and looking be straight in the eyes, he asks, "What do you know about this?"

Two pictures sit on the table before me, the first is a picture of my husband's car from his accident and the other picture is of Callie and a man I don't recognize. They appear to be sitting on the ground at a park, both with head injuries.

Nash asks again, "what do you know about this?" I tell them the truth, "my husband was in an accident a few nights ago and that I don't know anything about Callie and her friends incident."

He wants to know where I was yesterday evening, the time of Callies attack. "Clearly, I was right here" I explain. "I have a condition that doesn't allow me to leave the house, so I am always here."

Officer Nash and his partner glares at me like they don't believe me.

Putting the pictures back into the envelope, both officers immediately begin firing questions at me. Their voices overlap, one accusation tumbling over the next until it's impossible to focus on any single one.

"How do you know Michael?" one of them demands. "We tracked your phone."

"When was the last time you were at that church?" the other adds.

"Do you know Charles?"

"We found your DNA."

"How long have you known Ethan?"

"Where were you? Where were you? Where were you?"

The questions come faster and louder, circling me like a swarm, making my head spin. My heart pounds in my ears as I press my hands against my temples, trying to block out the noise.

"**SHUT UP!**" I scream as loudly as I can.

The room falls silent for a moment.

"As you can see, I am not well," I continue, my voice shaking but firm. "You need to leave. Now."

They exchange a look, clearly unhappy with my response, but I stand my ground. I insist again that I had nothing to do with any of the incidents and that if they have any further questions, they can contact my attorney.

Without giving them time to argue, I usher them toward the door, holding it open, with a tight, forced smile.

"Have a nice day, officers."

The moment they step out into the hallway, I shut the door quickly and lock it behind them.

Chapter 38

Callie

Sitting in the hospital next to Marcus and Olivia, my head is still foggy from everything that happened. The details blur together when I try to replay the night, but one thing is crystal clear, I know who really hit us.

What I can't figure out is why Olivia was following me in the first place or why she was driving Ryan's car. I know she said she was protecting me but I am not buying that. None of it makes sense.

When did my life become so complicated?

First, I catch Jordan cheating on Marcus, and somehow, I'm the one left feeling responsible for their breakup. Marcus never blamed me, but that doesn't stop the guilt from creeping in every time I see the look in his eyes when his name comes up.

Then the men who assaulted me when I was a child start turning up dead, one after another. Each time the news reports another body, a knot tightens in my stomach. Their faces are burned into my memory, ghosts from a past I tried so hard to bury. Now someone else has made sure they'll never hurt anyone again… and somehow, that puts a spotlight on me.

For a while I was sure the police would come knocking again. I kept expecting flashing lights outside my house, questions I couldn't answer, suspicion in every glance. But they haven't been back since that night.

Which makes me wonder if they've shifted their focus to someone else.

And now this, one of my best friends attacking Marcus and me in the park, then standing here in this hospital room pretending she has no idea how it happened.

Nothing adds up. Every answer leads to another question, another lie, another piece that doesn't fit.

The more I think about it, the more unsettling it feels, like I'm standing in the middle of a puzzle where half the pieces are missing.

My eyes drift back to Olivia.

Is she the one responsible for everything that's been happening?

Following me?

Showing up at the right moments. Always knowing more than she should.

Something tells me I may never know the whole truth.

Chapter 39

Lynn

It's strange looking back on how easily a child can mistake attention and toys for love.

The memory is still so vivid in my head. I can see the church hallway as clearly as if I am standing there now. She was five years old and I was seven.

The fluorescent lights buzzing overhead and the faint smell of lemon pledge. I watched my stepfather "Chuck" Charles Fields walk Callie down that corridor toward the library, with her hand in his.

My stepfather was taking another girl to his quiet room.

Jealousy didn't just sting. It clawed its way up my throat and burned behind my eyes. My chest tightened so hard I thought I might faint.

"I am his pretty little princess" I told myself. Why is he holding the new girls hand?

Seeing them together was more than my little heart could handle and I was going to do whatever I could to stop it.

My behavior shifted after that, or maybe it had always been there simmering.

My mom decided to home-school me because of my "issues." She didn't like my defiance. The way I was too rough and controlling with my little brother. She said there was something unsettling about the way I interacted with the family dog. She accused me of being cruel in the attention I gave and withheld.

There were other signs, things that as an adult I can no longer soften with excuses. Like the way I painted red figures on the bathroom wall to frighten my mom, or decapitate my dolls with clinical precision. In my small world, I could decide who was loved and who was punished.

At the age of sixteen, my mother enrolled me back into public school. She said I needed structure and normalcy. I became a sophomore at Mooresville High School, home of the Blue Devils. The irony wasn't lost on me, even then.

On the first day of school, I was in Art class waiting for the bell to ring. Palms flat against the cool surface of the desk, rehearsing the version of myself I would present to the rest of the school.

And then she walked in... It was Callie.

Ten years older then, but unmistakable. The same careful posture and the same innocent, wide eyes.

The girl from church. The girl who took his hand. The girl who took my step-daddy. The girl who ruined everything for me.

I did everything in my power to make high school hell for her and I don't plan to stop now as adults.

Last month, I saw her in person for the first time in eleven years and she pretended not to recognize me.

Her smile was controlled. Polite and professional.

But for half a second, just a flicker. I saw it. The calculation.

I hoped she would recognize me. I hoped her stomach would drop the way it used to when she opened her locker.

But now I don't need to put notes in her locker and now I am much closer than three rows back. And my plan is working...

Yes, I killed my stepfather. I waited one night when I knew he would be at the church alone, knowing he wouldn't be surprised to see me. After all, I have been trying for years to get his love and attention back.

But after hearing Callie talk about the way he touched her, everything changed. The betrayal cut deeper than anything I had ever felt.

How could he do that to me? I thought I was special.

When I confronted him, he barely listened. He turned his back and started walking away while I was still talking, dismissing me like I was nothing. Something inside me snapped in that moment. Years of anger, confusion, and hurt all came rushing to the surface.

Without thinking, I wrapped the rope around his neck. After his recent stroke, he was weaker than he used to be. Overpowering him didn't take much. But getting him up to the ceiling took more determination than I even knew I had. Anger can drive a person farther than they ever expect.

And the truth is... I don't regret it.

The other two men were different.

They weren't killed out of rage. They were part of a plan.

Chuck's death couldn't lead back to me, and the only way to make sure of that was to create a story the police would believe.

I needed to frame Callie. If the evidence pointed toward her, no one would think to look at me.

Ethan was the easiest.

Loosening three of the lug nuts on the passenger side of his car was easy to do while he was preoccupied in the bar.

Mikes incident required more patience. I had to track him down first, figure out where he stayed, learn his routines. He moved around constantly, which made it harder, but eventually I found him. From there, it was only a matter of timing.

He didn't have a car which made following him easy since he had to walk everywhere. Once I saw him go into the abandoned parking lot of the old mall, I knew it was my chance. I called to him by name, and as he turned to walk towards me, I pulled the trigger, then planted the drugs.

By the time I got home, the house was quiet. Daniel was fast asleep, never even noticed I had been gone.

And everything was exactly the way I needed it to be.

Epilogue

Callie

A pathological liar is not merely someone who bends the truth. She is an individual who exhibits a chronic, compulsive pattern of excessive lying. Such behavior that can cause significant distress and impairment in their life and relationship.

The lies are not sloppy. They are carefully and thoughtfully engineered.

I had done my research. I knew his reputation. The way he gravitated toward fragile women with fractured childhoods and haunted eyes.

He liked to believe he was rescuing them, gently excavating their trauma with soft questions and patient silence. He couldn't resist a damsel in distress.

So, I became one.

I gave him stories soaked in neglect and abandonment. I fed him just enough pain to keep him leaning forward in his chair, just enough vulnerability to keep his interest. I watched his expression carefully. The tightening jaw, the protective tone.

Every session, I adjusted the narrative. More darkness here. A softer confession there. Anything to make him invest.

Anything to put a wedge between him and Lynn.

Obsession is easy to manufacture if you understand what someone wants to believe. Daniel wanted to believe he was saving me.

What I didn't know.

What I couldn't have predicted.

Was that someone else was listening.

I had known Lynn was Jenna from high school the moment I saw her photograph on Daniel's shelf. The smile was older, but the eyes were the same. Cold and dark.

That's how I knew I had chosen the right therapist.

The past was already sitting in the room with us.

Yes, I lied.

Every word I told Daniel was completely fictional.

But I never imagined Jenna or Lynn would be listening to our sessions and I certainly never imagined she would start killing the men I mentioned.

The lies were supposed to create attention, not bodies.

I only wanted Daniel's focus. His divided loyalty. The slow disruption of his marriage. I wanted to watch him choose me.

I wanted control. I wanted to win.

By the time I realized what was happening, it was too late. The pattern was already forming, the news reports, the eerie similarities, the tightening timeline. Accidents that weren't accidents. Coincidences that weren't coincidences.

The police eventually tied Lynn to all three murders. Digital breadcrumbs and security footage connects her without question. Her attorney announced she plans to claim insanity.

The media moved on quickly once they had their villain.

Olivia was arrested for the attacks on Marcus and me. They found her finger prints on the tire iron that she threw into the woods. She served three months in jail and will have one year on probation.

Daniel lost his therapy license.

An internal investigation revealed he had been having inappropriate relationships with more than one of his patients. Confidential boundaries blurred and ethical lines crossed. His carefully constructed reputation collapsed overnight.

It wasn't how I imagined it. I hadn't planned for prison sentences or funerals or revoked credentials. I hadn't meant for the fallout to be this complete.

But in the end, I suppose I did win, and isn't that the only thing that really matters?

About the Author

I grew up in Homestead, Florida, with my parents and two brothers. I chose to leave my brothers out of this story because my experiences were different from theirs, and it isn't my place to tell their stories. Aside from that small detail, the therapy sessions described in this book are based on actual events from my childhood.

Although my parents didn't always make the best decisions for me and my brothers while we were growing up, we all turned out fine. When grandchildren came into the picture, my parents changed in the best way possible. They loved their grandchildren unconditionally, and for the first time, they began expressing that same love openly to us kids as well.

Today, my brothers and I can laugh about the crazy stories from our childhood. Without those stories, I wouldn't have the sense of humor I have today.

Rest in Peace, Mom and Dad, your love will always live on with us.

My husband, Chris, and I met in South Florida, and without his love and support, I would not be where I am today. I am incredibly grateful for the life we have built together and for the many experiences we have shared along the way.

In 2005, while I was pregnant with our third son, we made the decision to move to Mooresville, North Carolina, where we still live today and proudly call home. I currently work as an administrator of an assisted living community, a role that allows me to continue caring for and advocating for others. Before stepping into this position, I spent twenty years working as a nurse, a career that shaped who I am and strengthened my passion for helping others.

Being a mom to my three incredible boys: Cody, Colin, and Caden, will always be my greatest flex. You are my everything, and I am so proud of the men you are becoming. Always strive to be the best version of yourselves, stay true to who you are, and never be afraid to chase your dreams. As you already know, I will always be your biggest cheerleader. I love you more than words can ever express.

Also by Chrissy Stein-Martin

Coming Soon

Intrusive Eyes

A psychological thriller about a fifteen-year-old boy who prefers watching people instead of talking to them. From the safety of his bedroom window, he studies his neighbors, memorizing their habits, schedules, and weaknesses. Watching them makes him feel powerful and in control. But control is only an illusion.

The Truck Stop Killer

A psychological thriller where truck stops are never empty at night, the trucks glow under flickering neon lights, but danger waits in the shadows. One killer moves unseen, striking strangers with brutal precision, leaving only fear and blood in their wake.

www.ingramcontent.com/pod-product-compliance
Lightning Source LLC
LaVergne TN
LVHW041111150826
845673LV00007B/2011

* 9 7 9 8 9 9 5 3 4 3 4 0 0 *